S0-DFI-652

Another Redstripe, Please

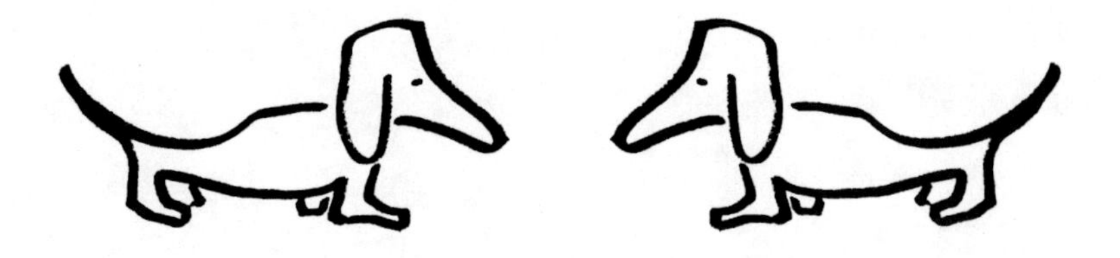

Dachshunds in the Midwest

Another Redstripe, Please

Dachshunds in the Midwest

By Jack Magestro

Unlimited Publishing
Bloomington, Indiana

Distributing Publisher:
Unlimited Publishing LLC
Bloomington, Indiana

http://www.unlimitedpublishing.com

Contributing Publisher:
Jack Magestro

Cover and book design by Charles King. Copyright © 2004 by Unlimited Publishing LLC. This book was typeset with Adobe® InDesign®, using the Myriad® and Adobe Jensen® typefaces. This book makes use of one or more typefaces specifically licensed by and customized for the exclusive use of Unlimited Publishing LLC.

First edition.

Copies of this fine book and others
are available to order online at:

http://www.unlimitedpublishing.com/authors

ISBN 1-58832-094-4

Unlimited Publishing
Bloomington, Indiana

For my wife, Jill,

my best fan.

Negril Beach, Jamaica— 2000 and Something

WE WERE back in Negril, one of our favorite places, and I was wandering alone along the seven miles of beach on an early June morning. The sun was just up and casting shadows of trees onto the sand as I strolled along in the ever-perfect air under a clear sky. The ocean was still calm and had not yet woken to cast any waves up onto the beach. Shirtless and shoeless, I wore a loose pair of old cotton shorts; superfluous, actually, other than to have pockets for my lighter and cigarettes. It was, to steal an often-used phrase, another perfect day in paradise and I was already thinking of my first beer.

Not many people were on that stretch of beach so soon after sunrise, but there were a few diehard young women lying atop towels spread on lounges, their skin soaked in tanning oil, doing their best to acquire skin cancer. I believe that they did not think or believe that some day, after thirty years of basking in the sun, they would all look like horse saddles. The bottles of designer water, stuck in the sand next to each one may have been able to keep them hydrated, but in the end, the sun would win and their youth would fade prematurely.

Besides a few wild dogs, some arguing birds and the leftover litter from the late partying of the night before and me, the only other things on the beach were some sleeping young men, curled on their own lounges or even just lying in the sand and sleeping off the excitement, ganja and high proof rum from the previous evening. I thought back thirty years to when I was twenty, as many of these reclined bodies seemed to appear to be, and wondered if I'd missed something by working so hard at odd jobs during that time of my own life just to pay for school and find a career. I didn't remember snoozing on a beach back then. The memory of my career was a little fuzzy that morning. I concluded that I *had* missed something, shrugged to my self and continued strolling.

While my wife was sleeping late as usual under a simple single sheet back in our rented cabin and dreaming her early morning dreams, I remembered the Redstripe tales told to us nearly a decade ago on that same beach in Negril. Over some time and several trips to the area, we met and continued to meet a local rastamafarian named Cirtron. He'd told us the story of Redstripe, a little dachshund, his girlfriend Sheila and his adventures with the little dog. The stories were somewhat unbelievable. He'd told us of sneaking the dog through international airports, how the dachshund wreaked havoc with the locals and how tiny Redstripe had charmed everyone she met in both Jamaica and the United States. My wife Jill and I often thought that maybe these stories were the product of the overuse of a certain prevalent drug in Jamaica, usually inhaled through the lungs, but the stories have remained with us for years. Thinking about them, I began to laugh out loud as I continued down the beach. No one cared that I was laughing at seemingly nothing, most everyone around was somnolent anyway and there are much weirder things to be seen on the Negril Beach than some middle-aged man walking along and laughing to himself.

I stopped for a moment to light a cigarette and to contemplate a pile of discarded conch shells. The pile was under a palm tree just outside a little shack that had a crude, hand painted sign stuck in the sand. The black letters listed conch, conch soup, jerked pork and chicken, and breakfast. One did not know what the *breakfast* really was, but the place apparently was selling it. The pile of discarded shells must have been three feet high and would have been worth a fortune back in the United States; the larger intact shells to be sold to adorn expensive coffee tables in affluent homes sporting the latest in interior design. To the Jamaicans, it was just a pile of refuse waiting to be buried in the sand.

The sun was beginning to make its way higher into the morning sky and I could feel it begin to sting my unprotected shoulders. I figured it was time to head back to the cabin and my sleeping wife and maybe find a cup of blue mountain coffee. I dug a hole in the sand for my cigarette with my bare foot, covered it and turned to make the trek back. I had only taken a few steps when I was confronted by a wandering beach vendor. He was selling aloe leaves and I, being one of the only moving objects on the beach, was his target.

The man, a very dark Jamaican—yellowish whites of eyes, enlarged feet from a life of pounding sand barefoot and wearing a only simple pair of khaki shorts—carried a large net bag over his shoulders crammed with aloe leaves. Actually, a better description of these would be aloe *branches*. These plants, the juices of which were applied to sunburn and were quite effective in relieving pain, grow to be six feet tall in Jamaica. The bag of branches looked like a bunch of truncated, handless green arms. The man stopped in front of me, placed the bag on the sand and made his pitch.

"Ya, mon. Your shoulders be getting' de red, mon. I have de aloe for you. Good for de burn. Very good."

I stopped and then realized I'd made a mistake. The word "no" or "no thank you" only works to decline an offer from the beach vendors if you keep moving. And one should never say "maybe later." The vendor will take that literally and pursue you "later" for the rest of the day or even the next. But regretting my error in stopping, I had only the second option left in order to remain polite and respectful.

"Maybe later," I said.

"Ya, mon. Irie. Y'come to our place and we rub in de aloe for you later. Come, I show you where t'go, come on, mon. Den you come back later." He picked up the bag.

Darn it. I was going to have to be rude in order get out of this one. I had no intention of going to "his place", wherever that was, just to be pressed to buy who knows what. I opened my mouth to say that I just needed be left alone but I stopped on the inhale before I spoke. I looked a little more closely at the man as I held my breath, wary and surprised at what I saw.

The Jamaican's beard and dreadlocks held some grey. And there were some new lines and crinkles around the eyes. Some gold adorned an ear and eyebrow that I did not remember. But I did remember the face, wiry frame and accent. It had been a couple years, but I would have recognized Cirtron anywhere.

"Cirtron!" I said.

"What? How be it dat . . . Ah! Ya, mon! Jock and Jeel! No! Can't be so!"

"It's me, Cirtron, remember? Jill's back sleeping at the cabin."

Cirtron actually did a little dance. He pumped his arms and stomped from one foot to the other while I thought about coincidences. "Jock and Jeel! No! Cannot be! Ya, mon, I remember. Redstripe!"

"Redstripe indeed, my man. What the heck are you doing here trying to sell me aloe when I can take two steps off the beach and break off a piece by myself for nothing?"

"I dunno," Cirtron grinned at me. "I do de stuff on de beach, mon. Sheila; she does de stuff in de house.

"Sheila?" I asked. "Sheila is here? What house?"

"Ya, mon. We have de guest house and all dat. De people come and stay and we make de living so. Ah! Happy times, mon!"

While my mind was awash in the waters of deja vu, I tried to concentrate on that last part. Cirtron had a house? And his girl friend, Sheila from New York was taking care of it? Something didn't fit here. I could feel invisible antlers, nourished by curiosity, growing out of the sides of my head. I wanted to go back and tell Jill that I'd found Cirtron. But I also wanted to know about Sheila and this "house." Was this just another story woven in the smoke of Cirtron's favorite vice?

"Cirtron, can you show me?"

"Ya, mon! Day all be dere. Sheila and Redstripe and Paris. I be take you, c'mon mon. Say, mon, have de extra cigarette?"

I reached into my pocket, shook out a cigarette from my pack and handed Cirtron a lighter. Nothing changes, really, over time. Cirtron was still bumming and I felt grateful that it was too early for him to have me buy him a beer. I would have gladly if I thought I could get explanations out of him in any hurry. Instead, we headed up the beach together and I had a feeling that the Redstripe stories would begin again and I would find the answer to the puzzle.

Another Redstripe, Please

Letters and Lawyers

Cirtron, Sheila's friend who she met in Jamaica, had left New York. Sheila, and the two little dachshunds, Redstripe and Paris remained after the airport adventures. The DEA would never forget the mess they had experienced with the little dog Redstripe. The confusion created when the long little hound took a liking to a drug dealer because he had gravy on his pants had caused a series of events to unfold. The ensuing events had become troublesome to all in the government agency. Most of the people at the facility in the hills ended up having to own up to questions that were tough to answer. Early retirements were in order.

Redstripe had been a stowaway with Cirtron, who was on his way from Jamaica to visit Sheila in the big city. But the little red miniature dachshund and Cirtron the rastamafarian parted company when Cirtron left New York and left Redstripe with Sheila. But they were only separate for a little while. The reunion would have its own set of complications.

Sheila spent some quiet times with Redstripe and her mom, Paris, in Sheila's little brownstone apartment. Sheila's days were spent at work at the insurance agency while Redstripe and Paris did whatever it is that dachshunds do in the house when no one is around. Most times, Sheila returned to peace. Many times, she did not.

Paris and Redstripe had one favorite habit in which they engaged. Sheila was not always diligent in securing the trash. Boy, there is nothing better for a dachshund than to have several uninterrupted hours with the kitchen garbage. There were days that Paris and Redstripe "trashed" the place. They really did. And they did it well. Everyone, including dachshunds, should have a hobby after all.

But usually, after the leftover spaghetti, the regurgitated vegetable scraps and a couple of things best left unmentioned were cleaned up, Redstripe and Paris and Sheila spent most evenings curled in a pile on the couch watching television.

Paris liked the police shows. This certainly had something to do with the squad sirens and she loved to bark when the police cars howled down the streets in hot dog pursuit with their lights flashing. Redstripe liked the educational channels; anything with animals. Sheila began to think she should get a second television. She never seemed to get to watch what she wanted: Dachshunds have a way of getting their way and the television channel selections were no exception.

One early evening a call from the doorman came over the intercom. "Miss Sheila?"

"Miss Sheila?" The tiny speaker played the doorman's voice into the apartment. That set Paris and Redstripe to barking their fool heads off. "*RRRwoof! RRR WOOF WOOF. RRR WOOF!*"

Sheila rose from the couch and keyed the intercom switch.

"What?"

"*Rrrwooff! WOOF WOOF WOOF, RRWOOF!*"

"Miss Sheila?"

"Yes? What is it?" she answered again and then, "Paris! Redstripe! SHUT UP, both of you!"

"Miss Sheila, what was that? Is everything all right?"

"Yes. Never mind, what is it?"

"There is a gentleman here for you. He has a package—looks like some papers—says it's real important."

"Ok, send him up."

Sheila turned to her stereo dachshunds. "Go on. In your bed. We have company."

Neither dog moved.

"Honestly! Would you ladies go?!"

Predictably, they didn't, wouldn't and couldn't. After all, Paris and Redstripe were dachshunds.

The man with the package arrived, knocked, and Sheila opened the apartment door. What the fellow had in the package would change things in a major way for Sheila, Redstripe and Paris.

To begin with, the package had information indicating that a distant uncle of Sheila's had passed away. The rest of the details were lengthy and complex.

Guess which lady (with two dachshunds and a friend from Jamaica) was the only heir?

Yup and Ya, mon!

In the little town of Wautoma, Wisconsin, Sheila's distant uncle had spent his most of his days making his living on a small farm. He raised, bred and tended to a herd that was sold for meat and hides. John Armstead had held the farm during the last forty years of his life. He had raised a family with his wife, the late Clara Armstead. His four sons, but one, had taken off for various other pursuits as time had gone on. The last son, Peter Armstead, had stayed on. He took care of the books, made the purchases for feed and hired the help to take care of the herd as his father had aged and had become unable to manage the farm on his own.

The two men had fought, as sons and fathers do. Peter had never really wanted to farm to begin with. Numerous arguments speckled the history of their relationship. John had written Peter out of his will. Clara, Peter's mother, was already gone when John Armstead died so the older man's will stood as contrived.

Peter was actually relieved to be quit of the farm. He was not surprised at all when he received a call from the family attorney who quietly explained that his father had left him nothing.

Yet in some ways, it was still hard for Peter to pack and leave the farm. In spite of his reluctance to be a farmer, he did have affection for the herd, the barn cats and the various woodland creatures that would come to the back porch of the old farmhouse seeking food. He even had some thoughts about missing the local human characters that populated the bars, gas stations and feed mill of the little town. But Peter did leave. He left the farm with hopes of some better futures while still mentally packing a few regrets.

The papers that were brought to Sheila in her apartment did not really explain all of this business between her distant cousin Peter and his father. When the man with the package brought out all the paper work, he only told Sheila that she now owned a farm in Wisconsin. He suggested that his law firm could take care of disposing and liquidating the property should Sheila desire this. He said that he could take it out her hands and she would not have to worry herself about the entire affair. A sizeable check would be delivered when all was said and done.

Easy. Just sign here, please.

Sheila, being Sheila, wanted a second opinion.

"Hey, girls!? You want to live on a farm for a while? Paris, Redstripe. What do you think?"

Paris and Redstripe came galloping into the room. The man with the suit stood up and said, "Do they bite?"

"No," said Sheila, "At least not often."

Redstripe and Paris were sniffing at the man's cuffs, "Would you like our firm to handle this for you?" the man asked with a little tension in his voice. He stared down at the circling hounds.

Sheila said, "I'll tell you what. You leave all the papers here and I'll read them and talk it over with Paris and Redstripe."

"Excuse me?"

"I'll decide after I talk with the dachsies."

The man left, confused. Redstripe, Paris and Sheila settled on the couch. There was no peace until Sheila clicked the television remote to "Rescue 911" so that Paris could watch. She asked the two again. "Want to see some cows?"

They both looked up, raised those dachsie eyebrows as if to say, "Cows? What Cows? Why would we be interested in cows?" They stretched their little jaws in wide yawns.

Sheila looked through the papers that night while sitting on the couch; a dachs under each arm. As far as she could tell, the man was correct; she now owned a farm in Wisconsin and there was enough money invested by her distant uncle that would provide returns to make a decent life on the old place.

Could she leave New York?

You bet.

Maybe she could even get a second television out of this. Sheila was really tired of not being able to watch the ten o'clock news.

Sheila, after phone calls she made to the offices listed in the papers she had received, decided to plan a trip to the farm in

Wisconsin, "just to see" before she made any drastic decisions. But before she had thought this all out, she received a phone call asking her to come to the law offices of Merril and Fich to "Please help us bring closure to this issue, if you may?" A moderate retainer had been afforded the law firm by Sheila's uncle's estate so they were moderately polite.

Sheila did make the trip to Merril and Fich. So did Paris and Redstripe. The elevator ride up was quite a travail for both dogs. As they little car began to rise, the dogs felt the upward motion and squatted down in nervous anticipation of what would come next. They both expressed their discomfiture in liquid fashion on the elevator floor.

The dogs and Sheila entered a room with dark wood paneling. Lots of books filled shelves and a vague smell of cigar smoke hung throughout the room. This was after a receptionist said in most certain terms that the two dachs could *NOT* be allowed in the back office and she did not even understand *HOW* those two *CREATURES* could have ever been allowed in this building to begin with and . . ."

Sheila said "Sweetheart, these dogs are with me, they are dachshunds and they do as they please. Why don't you chill out and get a date who gives you something else to think about other than to give your bosses' clients a hard time?"

"Well, I never!" exclaimed the receptionist disgustedly.

"That doesn't surprise me, honey." Sheila replied. The dogs started to attempt to excavate the carpeting.

After that, all was explained to Sheila about the farm in Wisconsin by the attorney in a back, cigar- and leather-smelling office. Redstripe and Paris had made certain that they left their impression in that office as to what they thought about the whole thing. Sheila signed all that needed to be signed.

When Redstripe, Paris and Sheila returned to brownstone apartment, Sheila made a final and brave decision; they would go to Wisconsin.

"Redstripe, Paris!"

The dogs looked up, eyebrows in little tents of anticipation. "Woomf?"

"What do you say we get in touch with Cirtron? You know, YA MON!"

"Woof, rrooff wwwoofff!"

"Yes, I thought so. You two are suckers for a good looking man! I am too."

For Sheila, there was a lot to do. She had to make plans to pack up the dogs and their toys and their bed (not that they ever really used it.) She had to get hold of Cirtron, sub-lease the apartment and deal with her furniture. Moving from the east coast to the center of the country was more of a job than Sheila had really thought about when she had made the decision to go to her late uncle's farm.

Cirtron was first. She wrote a letter to a post office box in Negril. It read:

Dear Cirtron,

> *You always told me you loved animals. Well, guess what! I have a FARM. You know, like cows and pigs and chickens and stuff; just like you have back home. And it is MINE! Redstripe, Paris and I are getting ready to go there. Want to come? The girls are excited to see you again and I think it would be fun. Write or call me collect and I will make the arrangements to get you there.*

Love, Sheila

Cirtron called a few days later. The phone rang in the evening and Sheila accepted the charge. "Hello?"

"Aie, Sheila, m'lady. Waht be happn', girl?"

"You got my letter?"

"Ya, mon. De letter, she be wid me here now. Waht be it wid de farm, girl? Since when be it dat you know how to take care of de animals and so? Big job, de y'know?"

"Well, I thought you could help. I mean, how much work can a couple of old cows take? Are you going to come or not?"

"Ya, mon! I come. You send de ticket again and I be dere. But, m'lady, know what you do. De farming , she be a lot of work, mon. Ah, my uncles, day say as much, mon. Y'know?"

"Cirtron, I'll send the ticket and some money. Pick it up at the airport in Montego Bay, ok? When you get to Chicago, you can take a bus up and meet me in Wautoma. I'll get a reservation at a hotel and put that detail stuff in with the money and ticket. You don't have to worry about bringing the dachs this time. It should be an easy trip. So you'll you come?"

"Ya, mon. I be check at de airport for de ticket and such in a few days, Irie."

Sheila finished the conversation, "Redstripe, Paris? Say hey to Cirtron." She held the phone down to the two little dachshunds. They just stared at the receiver. "Common guys, bark for Cirtron. It's CIRTRON ! You know, ya, mon! Irie!"

Paris snorted and Redstripe wandered off. They wanted to make sure Sheila knew who was in charge. *Gee whiz*, they thought, *where does she get off telling us when to bark? Really!*

After all was said and done, Sheila decided to let the apartment go and gave notice to her landlord. He only asked if the dogs were leaving too and then said we would be glad to let her out of the lease. She made arrangements for her furniture to be removed by a firm that bought and resold furnishings as complete sets to those moving into new apartments and had come with little in the way of chairs and tables and such when moving freshly into the city. The losers in recent divorces made up most of the firm's clientele. Two men came to the apartment one day to inventory the contents and to get a signed contract. The furniture would be sold on consignment.

After being allowed upstairs by the doorman, they knocked on Sheila's door. The dachshunds responded in full voice, of course

Sheila opened the door but one of the two men said."Hang it a minute, lady, we don't do dogs much. Hey? And not especially viscous ones! Ya, know? My gawd, whadayou got in there?" The guys had heard the howls and barks and snorts and snarls of Redstripe and Paris through the door and now that it was opened, the full force of the righteously indignant hounds blared out into the passage where the men stood.

"Baby Dobermans. Is that a problem?"

The first man, Jake, turned to his partner Milt, rolled his eyes and turned back to Sheila."Oh, well, yeah. Y'got puppies? Um, yeah, well ya know, they sounded like big dogs. Hey, I mean, they won't like pee on our shoes would they? They don't bite, do they? I mean, we could come back, y'know?"

"I don't think that's necessary," said Sheila."I can lock them in the bathroom if you're afraid of puppies if you want."

"Hey Milt, you afraid of puppies?"

Milt shook his head no but he was not too sure.

The men entered the apartment with their clipboards and forms. They intended to complete the inventory quickly but Redstripe and Paris had other ideas.

The dogs barked and they pranced and they darted at cuffs. They ran from room to room, constantly under the two men's feet. They made certain to make noise. They made a lot of it. Neither man could hear the other over the constant din of barking dachshunds.

"HEY, MILT, YOU GOT THE COUCH?"

"ROOF" and "WWROOF!"

"WHAT?"

"THE COUCH, YOU GOT IT ON YOUR LIST?"

"ROOF, WWROOOF!"

"I'M NOT A SLOUCH, I'M DOING MY BEST!"

"NO! THE COUCH!"

"I'M NOT A GROUCH, IT'S THESE DAMN DOGS !"

"ROOF" and "ROOF" and "WWROOF!"

"LOGS? MILT, THERE'S NO FIREPLACE. DO YOU UNDERSTAND?"

"ROOF," scamper, "WWRROOF!"

Things went on like that for a while. Milt and Jake continued the inventory including Sheila's O'Keefe prints while Sheila let the dachshunds do their thing. She thought the whole process was a stitch and celebrated her opinion by pouring herself a glass of wine from a half full bottle in the fridge. Beverage in hand, she continued to watch the festivities with great amusement.

Finally, when Milt and Jake left, Paris and Redstripe jumped unto the couch, lay down on their backs, feet in the air, and feel asleep.

They were thinking, *Gosh, they had helped a lot, hadn't they?*

On the Way to Montego Bay

CIRTRON'S TRIP to Montego Bay was much different than his last. This time he did not have Redstripe with him to act as a foil to solicit favors. Most of his trip was made on foot and the free food and drinks were scarce and hard to find. But Cirtron did make it to Mo Bay and, as Sheila had promised, found money and a plane ticket in his name at the airport.

When he was preparing to leave his family home in the mountains of Jamaica, his uncle Basi approached while Cirtron was packing.

"Hey, mon, whaht you be doing now, mon?" asked Basi.

Cirtron stopped stuffing things into his gym bag, looked up, and answered. "Ya mon, I gonna be de farmer. I am go to raise de cows and such with Sheila. I will go to Wascoonseen."

Basi turned his head to one side and laughed. "Ah! Now when do you change to be de mon dat works so hard? You would not know on which end of de cow does de business. Stay here, cousin, you can be help me in de shop. Dere is plenty work, mon."

"No, mon, I already made de decision and promise. Whad I need is de ride down and out to de road. Ga will tell me 'bout de cows. Sheila has told me day would not be so much trouble."

Basi shrugged knowing there was no hope of ever arguing and winning with Cirtron. "Okay, collect de stuff and we go down again to Negril. From dere, you be on your own, mon."

Basi went to start the old tan Chevy. Cirtron joined him at the car, climbed in as passenger, and placed his gym bag in the back seat. Over the hot and dusty and narrow roads to Negril, Basi piloted the way with Cirtron and finally deposited him near Alfred's', the beach bar and grill so popular with both the locals and tourists. Basi turned the car and started the return trip to the enclave, family and his machine shop in the mountains. Cirtron, once again, stepped on to Norman Manley Boulevard and stuck out his thumb to find a ride to Montego Bay. Within the seven miles of road and beach that make up Negril, Cirtron had plenty of friends. It was only a minute or so before someone picked him up. The driver took him from Alfred's up to the small airstrip that marked the north end of town.

"Dis be as far as I go, mon," the driver said. "Luck and go with Ga, respect."

"Tank you, mon," replied Cirtron. He climbed out of the car and began the trek to Montego Bay.

Two days later after a couple of short rides and after sleeping on the roadside, with his gym bag as a pillow, Cirtron was still a third of the way away from Montego Bay. He was dirty, hot and tired. He almost did not notice the car that pulled to the side of the road in front of him. It was a taxi. It had the red plates issued by the Jamaican authorities that legitimized the owner's right to charge fares for transport. Cirtron did not have much hope for a ride in this case even though the car had stopped for him. He had no money to pay a fare.

The taxi had a passenger who leaned out the window and called back to Cirtron.

"Hey, guy, looks like you need a ride. Get in. It's on me."

Cirtron looked and saw a tallish, slender black man in the passenger seat of the cab. As the rastamafarian approached, the passenger could be seen to be of Jamaican descent but with close cropped hair and western style clothing. He wore a freshly pressed blue shirt, creased white trousers and his sockless feet were clad in expensive looking leather sandals. The sandals showed no sign of wear. A simple gold chain adorned his neck. He smelled of some lime-based cologne.

Cirtron said his thank you and climbed into the back seat.

The driver steered the car back on to the road and took off, a rush of gravel escaping behind the rear wheels. The passenger turned in his seat to face Cirtron in the back. "So, my man, where are you going? I'm on my way to the airport, so we can take you that far. The cab is paid for and I figured you needed a ride just by seeing you trudging along there."

"De airport, ya mon. Dat is where I go," said Cirtron.

"Good. That works fine. What will you be doing there?" asked Cirtron's benefactor.

"I be get de ticket and take de plane to Wascoonseen. Gonna be de farmer, d'know?"

"Wisconsin?" returned the slim man, "Yes, I know that. It's a state in the Midwest of the United States around the Great Lakes. Actually I know the United States pretty well. I went to school there. I graduated from Yale a while back."

"Yale?"

"Yes," the man explained, "That's a big university in the United States. But I didn't like it there and came back here. I opened a Jet Ski rental business on the beach in Negril and right now I have to go back to the states to do some business with the manufacturing people. They've been sending me some units that just are not up to par so I need to go and speak with them."

Cirtron was intrigued. "So, mon, you be Jamaican? You d'not sound so. But you did de big school in de United States? Why come back here again?"

"Like I said, I didn't like it; too many people that are too selfish. I've found I would rather live here and make what living I can and enjoy my life with the people here. Let me tell you something. I have seen both sides of a lot. And compared to the Americans, I prefer our own countrymen. Jamaica may not have all of the things that are in the United States, but I believe our people are better, simpler and therefore actually more civilized. I don't mean to be negative about the states; I just prefer to be here. And let me tell you something else. I have come to understand that using one's head and not expecting more out of life than one deserves is the key to a good life. The Americans don't generally understand that. They can't think straight for worrying about wants they do not need. On our island, my friend, that problem is not so frequent. It's all about an attitude, really.

And I have learned this as well. It applies everywhere, here and in all of the other places to which I have traveled. It is this, *Common sense is not common.* Remember that."

The man and Cirtron continued their conversation during the last miles of travel to the airport in Montego Bay. Cirtron carried very little of the exchange. The man had lots of opinions to share. At one point, the man extracted a pack of Marlborough Reds from his shirt pocket and offered a cigarette to Cirtron.

Cirtron accepted reluctantly. "Ah, mon, jus de one. Day c'make you sick, mon. I be stick with de Ganga. Irie." He accepted the cigarette regardless and then a light and sat back in his seat, blowing smoke to the side and out the window of the car.

A bit later, the cab pulled up to the entrance to the terminal at the airport in Montego Bay and allowed the passengers to get out onto the hot pavement. The man and Cirtron shook hands, touched closed fists, respected and took off on their separate ways.

Cirtron would remember to tell Sheila about common sense. In the meantime, he made his way into the terminal, collected his ticket, cashed in Sheila's Western Union transmission at the bank exchange and made his way to the gate for his flight back again to the United States.

A Plane and Bus with Little Fuss

THE PLANE trip to the United States was without problems for Cirtron. He slept most of the way, snoring and missing most of the scenery viewable from his window seat. With a brief layover in Newark, New Jersey, the trip ended peacefully at O'Hare in Chicago. From there, Cirtron would need to find a bus to take him up to Wisconsin and the rendezvous planned with Sheila and the hounds in Wautoma. Once off of the plane and through customs, (no need to stop at baggage claim as all he had was the gym bag) he stopped the first official looking person he could find.

"Excuse me please. Can you tell me t'find de bus dat take me to Weescoonseen?"

Cirtron's person of choice turned out to be a janitor. He answered Cirtron. "I don't know much about busses, buddy. I just swing a broom and empty the trash. But you might ask at one of the information desks."

Ah, I tank you, sir. May I ask de question on how to get dere?"

"Oh, let me see. Follow this hallway, about fifty yards, take the second right after the *Newstand and Skyway Book Shop* and then the next escalator down. I think there is an info place at the bottom. Just ask there."

"Esculatar?"

The man looked at Cirtron, puzzled. "Yeah, buddy. You know. Those moving stairs things."

"Ah,yes. Ya, mon. I know of dese from before. Tank you. Go with Ga. Irie."

The man stood a moment in front of Cirtron hoping he'd been understood, but surprised by the answer. "Say, you're not gonna hand me a flower or something, are you?"

Cirtron did not get this, but just said, "No, mon. No flower today."

The rastamafarian followed the janitor's directions. As he passed the *Newstand and Skyway Book Shop,* a small book in the window caught his eye. The brown cover had a caricature of a dachshund on it below the title. It reminded Cirtron that he was on his way to meet up with Redstripe and Paris, and of course, Sheila at the end of his trip. He passed the window and quickened his pace, in a hurry to find the bus.

As promised, Cirtron found an information kiosk at the foot of the escalator. After some discussion, (the Jamaican dialect and the Chicago accent make communication difficult) he had enough information to be able to proceed to a bus route for Milwaukee and where to buy a ticket. Route number and ticket in hand, he left the lower doors of the airport concourse and stationed himself beside the correct sign as explained by the lady behind the desk. When a bus with the correct number hissed to stop in front of him and the doors opened, he climbed on. He handed the driver the requested ticket and then asked. "Ya, mon? Dese bus, she go to Weescoonseen? To Wautoma?

The driver answered. "No, not actually. But I turn around in Milwaukee. When we get there, you come and see me and I'll be sure to get you to the next route. Go sit down. I'll be sure to watch for you. OK?" The driver looked at the ticket. "Look, you've got a transfer in Milwaukee, piece of cake."

"Ya, mon," said Cirtron. And then, "I do not have de flowers, mon."

The driver had no idea how to respond to that so he just repeated, "Go sit down. I'll get you where you need to go." A few other passengers clambered on, the driver looked out to see that the curb was empty, he turned the wheel, applied the gas and left the airport.

An hour and a half later, in the bus terminal in downtown Milwaukee, the bus stopped and the driver directed Cirtron to the next route with a new driver both bound for central Wisconsin.

The Highway of Harrowing Hounds

SHEILA HAD packed her little white Toyota Camry, installed Paris and Redstripe into the back seat of the car and began the road trip to Wisconsin soon after the apartment was emptied. The lease papers had been signed and turned over to the landlord, the attorney's documents concerning the farm were in the trunk and a map, the route marked in pink, lay on the passenger seat. Sheila had called ahead to find some dog-friendly motels along her route to the Midwest. She planned to leave the city on Interstate 495, cross New Jersey and then pass into Pennsylvania. She would then take Interstate 80/90 all the way to Wisconsin. Redstripe and Paris had ideas about traveling of their own. The back seat was not part of them.

The trip became torture. The two dachshunds insisted on climbing into the front seats and to compete for Sheila's lap as she tried to drive and watch traffic. When shooed back into the rear seats, they tried to dig holes into the upholstery as if to hollow out holes in dirt to make comfortable dachshund beds. The windows became smudged with nose marks, nearly opaque in places and passing truckers blowing their huge air horns to warn the distracted Sheila out of the way only served to bring on the howling and baying of the hounds. Paris and Redstripe scrambled about the interior of the car, got under Sheila's feet and their claws punched holes and tears in the road map at her side making it useless.

Sheila was becoming frantic. She glanced down at her trip odometer and was dismayed to see she'd traveled only fifteen miles.

Rather than become one human and two dachshund fatalities, an accident just biding its time, Sheila knew she had to do something. She pulled off the expressway and into the first travelers' rest stop she could find. As she decelerated down the ramp to the stop, she noted a sign:

NO PETS

This was not turning out to be a good day, no, not at all.

Sheila parked the Camry and climbed out, careful to shut the door without pinning curious dachshund noses but closed firmly to keep the hounds inside. Stepping back around to the trunk, she opened it and then opened one of her suitcases. Extracting bulky items like sweaters and heavy jeans and leaving the light shirts, underwear and such behind, she took the items forward and opened the passenger door. Shoving the two dogs into the back seats with one hand, she used to clothing to stuff into the spaces between and around the seats. She was trying to construct a sort of dachshund dam. She remarked to herself that the interior of the car looked a little like a Chinese Laundry, but she hoped the barriers would hold.

With the trunk closed, Sheila returned to driver's seat, keyed the ignition and rolled out of the rest stop and back on to the highway. The dogs were not amused by the new arrangement and proceeded to whine and paw at the barriers of Sheila's wardrobe.

"Damn!" said Sheila.

"Woof!" said the dogs.

"Redstripe, Paris! Knock it off! You two need valium or something. Settle down!"

Humming down the highway, dogs trapped, for a while anyway, in the rear, Sheila knew she had to take another step. She adjusted the rearview mirror downward so that she could see the hounds still scrambling around in the back. Maybe some music would help; but nothing too exciting. Sheila reached over and fumbled in the glove compartment for a CD she was pretty sure had been tossed in there and forgotten. It was an album given to her by a long-ago cheesy date of hers who was a bank teller who thought he was a high-roller investor. She plucked the CD from the box, flicked open the case and chucked it into the player on the dash. The voice of John Denver filled the car. Either soothed by the ballads or just bored, the hounds settled down. The music worked but Sheila would be able to write down every word of every song from every track from memory by the end of the trip.

Crossing the rest of New Jersey was peaceful. Sheila continued and made it all the way to Pennsylvania, crossing over into that state near Stroudsburg. She stopped to feed and water the dogs and let them stretch at another traveler's stop near White Haven that did not have the dreaded *NO PETS* sign. Just before the stop, Sheila had seen a billboard that advertised an up class restaurant named *Casa Belle*. She thought the add looked nice. But the name seemed to have struck a memory somewhere within her mind. There was something about the word *Belle* that seemed familiar and she thought maybe it might be from something told to her by Cirtron when he was visiting in New York. But the feeling faded.

White Haven was near the edge of the Pocono's, a famous spot for romance and honeymoons. Sheila thought, ruefully, that the dachshunds were probably not the right company with which to enjoy the area. But even with her map destroyed by the marauding canine occupants of the car, she recalled that she had found a *Days Inn* in New Columbia that allowed pets. The three of them made it there in the early evening of a June day. She stopped the car in the motel lot, killed the engine and John Denver was mercifully silenced. Redstripe and Paris were not silent at all. They were suddenly up and ready for more adventures. The next adventure would have to be a walk on leashes on some of the grass on the edge of the parking lot.

Redstripe and Paris relieved, Sheila did the best she could to untangle the leads and headed the dachshunds into the lobby and up to the front desk of the motel. The two dogs pulled at the leashes in two directions as Sheila made her way across the carpet as they were both interested in a different potted plant decorating the edges of the lobby. With a little coaxing, all three, Sheila, Redstripe and Paris made it to the registration desk. "Excuse me?" announced Sheila to the clerk behind the counter, "I need a room for the night and I understand you take dogs. I have two."

"Yes mam, we can accommodate you but there will be an extra deposit for the dogs. Let me check. I think we have a room available for pets on the first floor. Would two double beds be alright?"

Sheila replied; one arm still extended as the dogs tugged. "That's fine, where do I sign?"

The clerk, who probably did not need to shave more than twice a week, produced some papers after clicking on his keyboard for a bit and then peered over the counter at Redstripe and Paris.

"Are these the dogs?" he asked.

Sheila, the tired captain of the good ship of two dachshunds with the Chinese laundry cargo could not help but say, "No. I just borrowed these two so that I had something to hold on to while I checked in. My dogs are still out in my car."

"Oh," said the clerk. "But there are just the two?"

"Just give me a pen, here's my credit card."

Sheila made one more trip to the car. She retrieved her lightened suitcase and the dog dishes and steered the dachshunds to their night's lodging, room key in hand. Most of her clothes remained stuffed between the car seats.

The room was not bad. It had two big beds, a TV and a clean bath. The pictures on the wall would have sold at some sort of starving artist type art auction, but the place was livable. Sheila lifted the dachshunds onto one of the beds with her, lay back, clicked the remote for the television and tried to relax for a little bit. Paris took about two minutes before she padded to the edge of the bed and asked to be let down. Redstripe followed suit. Sheila lifted the hounds down only to have them paw at the edge of the bed a few moments later to be hoisted back up. And then down again. The hounds would not settle. Having spent most of her patience during the drive, Sheila rose, extracted the three pillows from the second bed, tossed them on the floor and said, "Here, you two. Make yourselves comfortable and stay put for a while, please?" The two hounds must have heard the edge of exasperation in their caretaker's voice and plunked down between the pillows. Even Redstripe and Paris knew that certain limits were not to be exceeded. Shelia reached for the phone book in the nightstand.

She found a pizza delivery place not far from the motel, phoned in and ordered a pizza and some soda and then paged through more of the phone book looking for pet stores. Someone, somewhere, must be able to advise her about safely securing the hounds in the car during the remainder of the trip. As things were going, Sheila, with her long blond and attention-getting mane of hair, would be bald by the end of the trip if she did not get things under control. She worried that John Denver might lose his effectiveness in the next several hundred miles of highway 80. A pet store on page 175 caught her attention, not far from the motel, and she decided to visit it in the morning while the hounds were snoozing. The pizza man arrived a little later with Sheila's order.

There was a knock on the motel room door and a voice filtered through, "Giovanni's, got an order here for room 115." The two dachshunds broke into open throttled voices; a cacophony of canine sounds, Sheila opened the door, purse in hand. As she tried to juggle the offered box in one hand and extract money to pay the guy, Paris made her way out between Sheila's ankles and out into the hallway. The pizza guy took the money and tip, turned and left. But Paris was loose.

Sheila hurriedly placed the pizza box on the floor, glanced back to make certain that Redstripe was still secure in the room, and took off after Paris. Paris was streaking down the hallway, a mimic of a furry brown space shuttle flying at weed top level aiming to leave the planet as soon as possible. Sheila was in desperate pursuit in a flash; pizza forgotten. "*Paris!*"

Breathless, Sheila caught up with Paris ten doors down as the dachshund was pawing and barking at the door of room 125. As Sheila slowed to a stop, the door opened and a fat woman wrapped in a towel stood in the opening. "Can I help you? Is this your dog? Is there a problem?" The smell of fast food, greasy burgers, wafted into the hallway which explained Paris's interest.

Sheila really wanted to say, "No, I just found the dog in the parking lot and thought I might get some exercise by chasing it up and down the hall."

But she restrained herself and just said," Yes, I'm really so sorry. She just got loose and took off before I even knew it. Please let me apologize, we've been traveling and I guess I am tired and was not paying attention. I am so sorry."

The fat woman told Sheila not to worry about it, it was ok, and that the little dog was sort of cute. Sheila grabbed Paris in a football grip, left as quickly as she could; the lady's towel was beginning to slip and Sheila did not want to be around for that. Walking back down the hall to her own room she was dismayed to realize she'd left the door ajar (lucky as she did not take the key) but where was Redstripe? Had she taken off through the open door? No, Redstripe had already chewed through some of the cardboard box containing the pizza and was happily lapping at the cheese and sausage on one side. Sheila's dinner would be limited.

"Damn!" said Sheila.

"Woof!" said the hounds.

The next day would *have* to be better.

The hounds and Sheila did make it through the night without further incident and although Sheila had to switch beds halfway through the night to get some room to sleep while the hounds controlled the first bed; the sun came up once again and the world looked ok. Sheila revisited the phone book in which she had been researching pet stores and snuck out of the room while the dogs were still snoozing under the covers of the first bed. The pet store was just blocks away and she figured the hounds would not rise; exhausted from traveling and from a little extra pizza from the day before. It was a three block jaunt and Sheila entered the doors of the pet store.

"Excuse me?" she approached the first person she found."I need a crate or a grate or something for my car for my two dogs. They are just bouncing all over my car and I'm afraid they will hurt themselves or get me into an accident. Do you have something?"

"Oh, sure," replied the clerk. What you need is a couple of harnesses. We have a bunch. What kind of dogs?"

"Dachshunds. Little ones."

"They come in more than one size?"

"Just show me, could you?"

"Oh, sure," the clerk led the way down one of the isles crammed with dog toys, leashes, collars and rubber chew thingys. "Here you go."

The clerk took a jacket like looking thing off of a hook and showed it to Sheila. It had a strap for around the chest of the dog and another for around the middle. The closures were of Velcro and there was a sort of a strap on the back. "See? You put this on the dog and the straps keep it in place, then the loop on the back is for the seat belt and keeps the dog from wandering. These are very popular."

Sheila did not hesitate, "I'll take two. Two small ones."

The items paid for and wrapped in a plastic bag, Sheila returned to the motel. When she entered the room, she could tell that Redstripe and Paris had never moved. Maybe the next leg of the trip would be better. She rustled the hounds out of their warm covers, took them outside for a bit, fed and watered them and then packed the Camry. The dogs bristled a bit when she applied the harnesses and clipped the dogs to the belts, but then she was back on her way to the west on Interstate 80. She'd grabbed a coffee, bagel and cream cheese from the motel lobby and munched as she drove, the dogs secure in the back seat. Just in case, Sheila started the John Denver CD once more. Ohio was not too far away.

Redstripe and Paris remained calm and quiet, secure with their safety harnesses and lulled into oblivion by the music coming from the dashboard CD player. Sheila herself felt pretty numb as she drove and listened to the CD. It may have been some sort of Rocky Mountain High thing influencing her as the sounds played into the car. The three of them crossed into Ohio near Youngstown and

Sheila figured she might still make it to Toledo if things went well. Then they hit the toll way. A road sign warned of the first set of toll booths coming up and that those without exact change should bear right. Sheila did.

As the Camry slowed to thread its way into the payment booth for the toll, Sheila felt a cold poke on her right elbow. She glanced down and right to see some of her clothes that had been used as a dachshund dam on the passenger seat and then at Paris who was trying to get her attention via nose signals. Paris was loose and in a moment Redstripe came scrambling up between the seats and over the broken clothing barriers as well. The two dogs, seemingly so quiet for so long during this current leg of the trip, had taken turns chewing at each other's back straps and broken themselves free while Sheila had been the victim of highway hypnosis. Redstripe and Paris were actually pretty proud of their accomplished jailbreak. Tails were wagging.

"Damn!" said Sheila.

"Woof!" said the hounds.

They pulled up to the toll booth. Sheila held the wheel with one hand and fumbled for her purse under the paws of the escapees and managed to grab some single dollars to pay the dollar and five cent toll. Paris and Redstripe began to howl, bark and attempted to cross Sheila's lap to get at the stranger in the toll booth. She nearly flung three dollars at the poor man and stepped on the gas to leave the booth while trying to shoo the dogs into the back seat. The barricade for the booth did not rise and the Camry, with Sheila's foot suddenly on the brake, lurched to a halt. The toll keeper leaned out of his window and shouted, "Lady! Your change!"

"Forget it!" Sheila yelled back. "Keep it and pay for the next car! Let me out of here!"

The barricade rose and Sheila, while still attempting to shoo the hounds, glanced in the rear view mirror to see the car behind her pull up to the booth and the toll keeper flinging his arms about while apparently trying to explain to the next driver. No matter, the Camry with all three occupants accelerated forward.

The Camry was low on gas, the hounds were loose and Sheila took the next exit off of the interstate to fill up and to find some way to re-secure the hounds. There was a "FEED AND FILL" just off the end of the exit ramp and she pulled in. Sheila climbed out of the car, careful to close the door on the hounds while leaving a window down enough for air and stepped back to the pump to fill the gas tank. Fifteen gallons later, purse over shoulder, she crossed the parking lot to the "FEED AND FILL" store to enter and pay for the gas.

At the counter, as she was paying, she asked "Do you have a stapler?"

"Staplers?" This very young clerk behind the counter was female and while shaving was never going to be an issue, she appeared as though it might be some time before she needed any underwear above the waist. "Uh, no. We don't carry staplers." She handed Sheila her change. "Sorry."

"I don't want to buy one. I want to borrow one. Do you have one or not?"

The young clerk replied, "Uh, yeah, I s'pose so. Let me check." She bent down and rummaged under the counter a moment and rose again and handed Sheila a stapler. "You're gonna bring it back?"

"Yes I will. I just need it a sec to staple my dogs. I'll be right back."

Sheila left the store while the clerk stood transfixed.

The stapler did a nice job of rejoining the chewed straps for the two dachshunds and within in a few moments Sheila had the disgruntled hounds re-installed safely with their harnesses in the back seat. She'd have to keep an eye on them to make sure they did no more chewing so she adjusted the rearview mirror once more so that she could see them from the driver's seat. Stapler returned, the two dogs and Sheila turned to the interstate in the Camry once more with the CD playing. Toledo seemed a long way down the road.

Sheila and the two dogs did make it across Ohio, then Indiana and further into Illinois before they turned northward toward Wisconsin. Rest stops, fast food places and motels all blurred into one collage over the next days. Thankfully there were no more escapes and no more motel fat ladies in towels or chases down unfamiliar hallways. But the trip took its toll on all three of them. They were tired. Even John Denver was beginning to sound a little weary although that may have been because the CD, playing on and on, may have been begun to wear. There was, however, one last problem that occurred at a fast food place somewhere in Indiana.

Sheila stopped at a burger type place, a chain, wanting to walk the dogs and use the facilities inside her self. A little food was in order for her and she figured she would share a little with the hounds even though it might be a little unhealthy for them. She paced the dogs on their leads on the grass on the edge of the parking lot and then secured them back into the car. She headed for the glass walled restaurant's doors. After using the ladies room, she approached the front counter and ordered a large hamburger and fries for herself, a drink, and a small hamburger she figured she would split between the two dachshunds as a treat. Returning to the car, she let the two dogs out, leashed, onto the parking lot, placed her own stuff on the driver's seat and then unwrapped the smaller hamburger and tore it into two halves. She placed it on the ground for the two dogs.

They nosed and just stared at the two halves of burger. They looked up at Sheila with quizzical expressions on their little faces.

"Oh, sorry, I forgot!" Sheila said. She reached down, removed the tops of the hamburger fragments and removed the pickles, popping the offending condiments into her own mouth. Dachshunds never eat pickles. The pickle less hamburger halves disappeared in about four bites each. It may have been less. It happened too fast to see. Sheila reached through the open window of the car for her own food and realized she did not have her purse. She'd left it on the counter when she paid for the food. "C'mon ladies, I have to go back inside or we won't have money to get to where we are going." Sheila, with the dogs still on their leashes, headed back to the restaurant in pursuit of purse intending to disregard any *NO PETS* rules in her haste to retrieve her purse.

She had not taken more than a few steps back inside the restaurant, dogs in tow, when an employee approached her and was holding her purse for her. "Ma'am? This is yours? You left it on the counter."

"Oh, thank you, thank you!" responded Sheila, "I don't know what I would have done . . ."

The person started to hand her the purse and said, "Don't worry, it happens all the time. We're just glad we caught you. But, um, the dogs? They really shouldn't be in here. Health regulations and all that."

"Hey, we are on our way. Thanks again." Sheila reached for the purse and somehow dropped Redstripe's leash in the process.

Redstripe, free of the constraint, took off and paddled after a man headed for the restrooms. The man pushed open the door and the pneumatic closer held the door ajar long enough for Redstripe to bound inside. Alarmed, not thinking, Sheila followed the little dachshund right inside the tiled room.

The dog skidded to a halt and Sheila, inside the men's restroom, reached down to grab the little hound. Two men, their backs to her and facing the wall doing what men do in men's restrooms swiveled their heads back and over their shoulders in unison to view the intrusion.

"Hey!" shouted the first. "What do you think you're doing?"

The second exclaimed, "Lookatthat! It's a wiener dog! Is it yours lady?"

Sheila replied, "Yeah, it's mine. Sorry." She left as quickly as she could, Redstripe in arms.

The employee with her purse was just outside the door and handed it to Sheila without a word. She retrieved Paris and the three of them left the site as quickly as possible. There might have been a little rubber from the tires of the Camry that was left in the parking lot.

Eventually, after passing through the maze of expressways around Chicago and then Milwaukee and then passing the towns in Wisconsin of Port Washington, Fond Du Lac and Oshkosh and even bizarre places like Omro, they arrived at a final motel in Wautoma. The three of them checked in and sleep was in order.

Bus Stop at the Lakeshore Family Diner

THE DRIVER turned his huge bus off of the county highway and into the parking lot of a medium sized diner. The sign, in neon, read "Lakeshore Family Diner———EAT." Cirtron rose up out of his seat, grabbed his gym bag, and made his way to the front of the bus. The other passengers ambled forward too.

At the front of the bus, Cirtron addressed the driver.

"I tank you, mon."

The driver looked back over his right shoulder at the rasta man. Cirtron chucked him on the shoulder with a closed fist. "Respect, mon!"

The driver just nodded and Cirtron climbed down the steps of the Greyhound bus and onto the asphalt parking lot of the diner. He took two big lungs-full of air, cold to him, and then looked at the entrance of the diner. In he went.

Once inside, he glanced left and right at the narrow passages lined by booths. A counter was right in front and he stepped toward it. He seated himself on a chromed, floor-anchored stool with a red vinyl seat. Cirtron thought the stool looked like a shiny red mushroom. Color notwithstanding, he was reminded of the much darker "shrooms" his uncles cultivated in the mountains of Jamaica.

One of the bustling waitresses came up to Cirtron right away. The plastic tag on her short sleeved shirt read "Mary." She was tall, dark haired and large shouldered. Her thick hair was pulled back by a single barrette. She smacked a green and white order form on the counter in front of Cirtron, placed her hands, palms down, on the counter and asked, "What do you need, Bob?"

Cirtron was confused and replied, "Ah, no. I'm not Bob. I be Cirtron."

"Well," said the waitress, "Ya' do look like Bob Marley."

Two stools down, a young man dressed in jeans and a flannel shirt glanced over and laughed, "Bob Marley! Ha, Mary, that's a good one!" He continued to chuckle as he clutched his fork with grimy fingers. "Bob Marley, yeah, that's good."

Startled, Cirtron chose to ignore the joke and looked up and down the waitresses' forearms. The left was hairy. The right had been shaved. On that right forearm he noticed a beautiful tattoo. The image of an eagle, peering out from some sort of multi-colored foliage, had been stenciled on the skin on the back of her lower arm.

Cirtron was intrigued. "Preety picture on de arm, mon! Where did it come from?"

"Oshkosh," stated Mary.

"Oshkosh?"

"Yeah, town about thirty miles from here. It hurt like hell when I was getting it done. Lots of bleeding."

"Ah," said Cirtron. "Sorry to hear dat, but it is de pretty thing t'see."

Mary leaned over the counter and said, flatly," I've got nine more, what will it be for you?

Cirtron did not see the other nine tattoos and did not ask about them.

"Coffee," he said.

Check In and Check Out

While Cirtron was sipping coffee, Sheila, Redstripe and Paris were pulling into the motel right next to the diner. By the time he paid the bill and said goodbye to the waitress, Mary with her tattoo, Sheila and the dogs were already settled and ready for an evening's sleep. Cirtron left the diner and made his way just next door to the motel.

Standing at the registration desk, gym bag in hand, Cirtron asked for a room for the night. The hotel manager eyed him a little longer than normal and then said, "Yes, we have rooms available. It's not a busy time. The spring fishermen have left and the summer tourists haven't showed up yet. Just one person?"

"Ya, mon. Just me."

"Okay, then, we'll put you in a room with two kings but we can just charge you for a single. That alright?"

"Ya, mon. Dat be fine. Not to worry 'bout the kings, though. I jes need to get de sleep alone, mon."

The manager blinked and paused but then recovered and said, "No, I meant the beds, the sizes. Never mind. Here," he handed a form to Cirtron, "just fill in your name, home address and the plate number on your car. I'll get you keys and a property map."

"Don't have de car, mon. The bus, she be de one dat bring me."

The manager took a breath and then explained, "Fine, just fill in the name and address and we'll get you all set." Cirtron took a desk pen, filled in Negril, Jamaica, West Indies and his name.

The clerk wasn't quite finished when he took back the form. "Do you have a last name?"

"Ya, mon," answered Cirtron. The last one I be using be Cirtron and still it be so. Does not change, mon."

"Right, ok, fine. How will you be paying, sir. We take Master Card, VISA, American Express and the Motel 'Merica credit card."

"Wid de money, sir. I use de money, irie?"

"You mean cash?" The manager looked down at the form and the address that Cirtron had filled in and asked, "You don't mean Jamaican money, do you? I'm afraid we might not be able to . . ."

"No mon, I have de *YOU ESS DEE* money from Sheila, d'you see?" Cirtron plucked a handful out of the gym bag.

"Do you mean U.S Dollars, sir? Is that what you have there? That would be fine." Cirtron paid, collected a map and key and a list of the amenities for the motel which included breakfast off the lobby in the morning and then made his way to his room. With the gym bag plopped down on the second king sized bed, Cirtron lay down on the first king sized bed, flicked through the cable channels on the provided television and fell asleep still clothed. The television remained on, casting stroboscopic colors on the motel room walls the rest of the night. Cirtron snored his way into a deep sleep. Sheila and the hounds snoozed away in another room just a ways down the hallway. While neither party realized the other had arrived in Wautoma, they would meet, accidentally, in the morning.

Cirtron was the first to rise. His internal clock was still set in Jamaican and it was always his habit to rise early. As the next morning's bright June sunlight began to sneak in around the edges of motel room's curtains, Cirtron was up and ready for a shower. Once clean, dried and dressed in clean clothes from the gym bag, he headed to the lobby to seek out some breakfast.

Sheila woke not too much later. It took her a while longer in the bath than Cirtron. She dressed, fussed with her long blond hair, and then shook the hounds awake so that she could get them on leashes and walk them. While Cirtron was piling toast, bagels and fruit on a plate at the breakfast buffet off the motel lobby, Sheila was out in the back of the establishment with Redstripe and Paris hoping they would get things over with quickly. They didn't; too many smells to investigate, but the three finally headed back in. The outside door near their room was locked. Sheila had to guide the hounds up front to the main doors to gain entrance. It was a bit of a walk around the building but the two dogs pedaled their little legs willingly all they way up to the main entrance.

Once indoors, of course, the dogs smelled breakfast. They began to try to drag Sheila by their leashes toward the side room with the buffet. Having inhaled most of his food quickly, Cirtron was just leaving the room. All four, two humans and two hounds, literally bumped into and tangled with each other at the doorway.

"Sheila!"

"Cirtron!"

"Ya, mon. It be good t'see you m'lady. See, I told you I would come t'here!"

Sheila let go of the two leashes and threw her arms around the rastmafarian and hugged him; her long blond hair tangling with his dreadlocks. She spoke into his shoulder. "You made it!" You found everything? How was the trip? Did you get the ticket and, well, I guess you must have, huh?"

"Ya, mon. But de dogs, mon. Day are in back to find dere breakfast. Maybe we go an catch de two?"

Sheila had not realized that as soon as she'd dropped the leashes, Redstripe and Paris, dachshunds that they were, had taken off to follow their noses to the closest food. They could be seen in the next room and could be heard whining around the chairs of a young couple with two preschoolers all seated at a table with their morning munchies. Alarmed, she entered the room to corral her hounds. Cirtron just dropped to the floor, crossed his legs and called out, "Hey, dere, you dogs, Redstripe, Paris! C'mon here you little ones. C'mon!"

Redstripe and Paris froze just a moment after, looking in Cirtron's direction and, amazingly, streaked right for him, loose leashes flapping behind. "Doggy?" said one of the little ones at the table. The mother shushed the child.

"Redstripe, Paris. Ah! Be it de good ting an see both of you both again, here!" The two dogs climbed onto Cirtron's lap and he embraced the two little hounds. They rose up on their hindquarters and began to paw at the front of his shirt in order to gain purchase and rise up to lick at the remains of recent breakfast still stuck in the Jamaican's beard. Sheila looked on and had to wipe one eye. Cirtron laughed while the hounds licked.

The woman with the Jamaican, two dachshunds and farm to be discovered in Wautoma, knelt down and tried to hug all three of her dearest friends. She rose, turned to the front desk and called to the day manager.

"Miss? I think we'd all like to check out now."

Realtor's Office

With Cirtron and the two dogs in the car Sheila, in the driver's seat, started the engine. She drove the little Camry out of the motel parking lot and out onto the county highway. The office for Egan's Realty was only a couple of blocks north. Sheila turned the car into the small lot in front of Egan's, parked it and shut off the engine. The lawyers in New York had told her that this agency was where she could complete forms and pick up the keys to the farm buildings on the property she had inherited.

Sheila, Cirtron and Paris and Redstripe piled out of the Camry. It was a bit of a leap from the back seats for the two little dachshunds. But they were excited and were down and out of the car before the humans had a chance to help them.

Paris and Redstripe scampered across the asphalt and up to the glass door to the realtor's office. It was trimmed with cheap-looking aluminum. Their little heads craned up, waiting for the door to be opened. Their tails were wagging. Dachshund eyebrows were raised and eyes were bright.

Cirtron looked a little worried. He asked, "Will day let de dogs into da building?"

"If we don't ask, they can't say no," said Sheila, and she stepped toward the door.

"Come on girls." Sheila opened the door and the dogs rushed over the threshold and into the small office. Sheila and Cirtron followed them in.

A woman in her late forties sat at a desk. Plastic-rimmed glasses lay against her chest, secured by a beaded string that was slung around the back of her neck. She wore a business jacket and skirt.

"Oh my goodness!" said the woman. "You can't bring those dogs in here! Please!"

Sheila looked at her and said, innocently, "I can't?"

Cirtron said, "Irie, it be okay, mon. Day jus' be de little dogs."

The woman seated at the desk sniffed and then reddened. Redstripe and Paris had already made their way behind her and both of the dogs were snuffling at the woman's nylon clad ankles.

"Oh my goodness!" she said as she lifted her feet from the floor and away from the dogs. She pushed her chair back from the desk, nearly rolling the wheels over dachshund ears. Leaning back, she raised her feet even further and away from the inquisitive hounds.

It was too far a lean and she went over backward in her chair. When she and the chair hit the floor behind the desk, the impact made a loud thump and the two dachshunds scrambled back toward Sheila. The woman lay on her back in her chair on the floor behind the desk. . Her skirted legs were spread, immodestly, toward the heavens. Cirtron looked up and concentrated on a spot on the office wall. As amused as he was with the entire situation, he did not want to seem disrespectful or too interested in the view.

The dachshunds began to bark.

"Hey, little dogs," Cirtron said, "be still, mon. be still."

Sheila walked around the desk and bent down over the woman.

"Are you okay?"

The woman's eyes were wide and she said, "Yes, I'm fine. Can you please hold on to your dogs? What was it you wanted?"

"Let me help you up."

"Uh, no, I'm fine. What was it I can help you with?"

Sheila said,"I was told your office has the keys to the buildings on the Armstead farm. I guess I am the new owner so I sort of need them. And I was told there were some papers I had to sign and deal with here in your office."

The woman remained on her back in her tumbled chair behind the desk and the dachshunds came back to investigate. Cirtron crossed his arms and looked at still another spot on the wall. The woman made no move to try to get up but eyed the two dogs."Can you please get these dogs away from me?"

Sheila shooed the two dogs."Go on, let this lady alone! Behave!" Paris and Redstripe looked up with an offended expression on both of their little faces. But they retreated.

The woman on the floor seemed relieved when the dogs moved off and then said,"The Armstead Farm? Um, I don't know much about that. Mr. Egan would, but he isn't in right now. But the caretaker? She could get you into the buildings. She has keys I think. That would be Ms. Carson. She lives right next door to the property and has been watching over things for a while. Just go see her, I'm sure she can let you in today and then you can see Mr. Egan about things tomorrow."

Sheila had one more question."Where exactly is this place, the Armstead farm?

The woman, still on the floor, lying back in her overturned chair, gave directions.

Then Sheila asked,"Please, can I help you up? Are you going to be alright?"

The woman said,"Oh no. Oh yes, I'm fine right here. Please, if you come again, please leave your dogs outside. I'll get up after you leave if you don't mind"

Cirtron and Sheila left the office. The dogs followed them out and over to the car. Everyone clambered in.

As Sheila started the engine again, she was thinking that maybe things would not be so simple. Cirtron was wondering why the lady in the office, seemingly so stiff and formal, had been wearing thigh-highs with lace undies. Redstripe and Paris decided they would both rub their wet noses all over the back windows as they peered out of the car.

Dachshund nose painting on glass is a much underappreciated art form.

The Armstead Farm

SHEILA FOLLOWED the directions given by the secretary in the Egan Realty office and together with the dogs and Cirtron, she made her way north. The Armstead farm that she had inherited was described as being only about a mile north of town. She found the gravel drive leading to the house easily by identifying the fire location number; a red sign with white letters on a steel post driven into the soil near the entrance to the property. She steered the Camry up the long stretch of drive and stopped. She did not think the place looked like much. Cirtron was ecstatic. He burst from the car while Sheila pushed open her own door slowly and stepped out to get a better look. Cirtron was nearly bouncing and the dogs climbed down and out onto the front lawn with no help, all on their own. Sheila grimaced. Those dogs were going to hurt their backs one of these days.

"Big house!" yelled Cirtron.

"Looks like it could use some work," said Sheila.

The house had been stained a brown color and looked in need of repair. While flowers grew against the foundation and the roof looked tight, gutters hung from the eaves at unhealthy angles. A section of fascia was missing at the edge of one part of the roof and the rafters stuck out like bad teeth. The window screens looked torn and rusty. A leaning shed adorned one side of the house, open on two sides and the grounds looked like they could use some cutting. The dachshunds were thrilled to be quit of the confinement of the car and galloped forward to explore.

Sheila and Cirtron became aware of a soft hum, rubber tires on soil, and the dachshunds stopped, turned and looked. A powered golf cart was approaching; a woman at the wheel. The cart was traversing a double rutted lane leading from the next property and quickly came to a halt near the drive on which the Camry was parked.

The driver, once stopped, stepped out slowly, the caution of age governing her movements. She wore a wildly printed house dress that ended at mid calf; the pattern looked like it had once been copied from a curtain in a Caribbean resort. She had a full head of white hair, short, cut off half way down her neck, thick glasses and a pair of clean Nike running shoes on her feet. She looked as though she must have weighed 180 pounds and could not have been more than five feet tall. "Well, hey there. 'Been expecting you. I'm Rose Carson, they call me Carson, and I'm the sorry wretch that has had to be watching over this place till someone showed up after old Armstead died and his son took off. Pleased to meet you." She extended a chubby hand and Sheila shook it.

"Hi, I'm Sheila, and this is Cirtron. We just got here. How did you know we were coming?"

"You're gonna want to corral those two little hound doggies of yours before they go too far. They could get out in the back and get stepped on by the herd. How did I know? Girlie, word travels around here like the flu. I just heard you were coming. Cirtron?" Carson regarded the rastafamarian and clasped his arm with both hands. "Welcome here, my friend. And don't let'm call you Bob!"

"I see," said Sheila. Cirtron went to catch the dachshunds.

"Well, girlie," Carson looked up at Sheila, noted her blond hair and looks but kept silent on what she thought about this would be rancher/farmer, "we'll see what you see. Let me take you into the house, I got the keys and some papers here for you in the go cart and we can get you acclimated. Better get your friend too. If he's staying, he's gonna have some work to do."

Sheila called to Cirtron who had a dachshund under each arm and the five of them headed for the front door. At the front entrance, Carson pulled some keys from a folder she had taken from the golf cart, opened the screen door, propped it with an ample hip and unlocked and opened the main door. She waved Sheila, and the hound holding Cirtron into the front room. "Welcome home," Carson smiled.

Sheila was not smiling but Cirtron's eyes widened as he looked around. Redstripe and Paris were wriggling to get free and sniff the place out.

Entering the front room, Cirtron squatted down and released Redstripe and Paris. They took off to examine the first area; noses snuffling around the edges created by the walls and floor while inhaling deep noisey breaths and snorting out short wet sounding exhales. The two of them moved almost too fast to be seen. Sheila gazed at the walls and the furniture.

The furniture, left behind by John Armstead, was bad enough: dark brocaded chairs and couches well-stained and with claw feet legs. It looked as though bears had been living in there and had used their claws to rearrange some of the fabric. Cushion material stood out in tufts and the fabric of the furniture was pushed up in wrinkles here and there like badly thrown bedspreads. The walls were worse. They had not been acquainted with a new coat of paint in what looked to be generations. As time had gone by in that front room and pictures had been added, moved and subtracted, large faded patches decorated the walls. A myriad of unused nails, pounded into the plaster, poked out nearly everywhere. The rugs on the floor had lost their colors and patterns long ago.

The dogs headed for the back room and Cirtron plunked down in a chair that was loosing its stuffing. "Ah, mon! Soft! Good!"

Sheila just stared. The two dachshunds could be heard scrambling and snooting around in the back room, the kitchen.

Carson looked at Sheila's expression and laughed. "Heh, heh, heh! I told you Cirtron would have some work to do, hey? And I haven't even taken you out back yet. That'll be a treat, let me tell you."

"Oh my god," said Sheila.

"Ya, mon, be it so cool!" said Cirtron.

"Heh, heh, heh," chuckled Carson.

At least the place did not smell as Carson had aired it when the weather was good, as it was now, and the summer breezes made their way into the house through the opened windows and rusted screens. The curtains were useless; so aged and thin that they were virtually transparent. But the air did flow. The hounds scampered back into the front room and leaped up to join Cirtron on his chosen seat. "Ya, mon, little dogs. D'you like?"

The two dogs woofed in excitement, expressing their approval of the new home. There would be lots of corners and things to sniff and explore but they were content for a moment to rest on Cirtron's lap.

Sheila was thinking that New York was a long ways back.

Rose Carson looked at Sheila who was frowning and looked at Cirtron, his yellow smile wide in his black face and thought for just a moment. She did want these two newcomers to be comfortable and to take over the farm; she was tired of looking after things. After all, an old lady had other things to do than watch over the neighbors and their animals and house. "Tell you what you two, you must be hungry. I wouldn't be surprised if the little doggies were too. I can take you out to the pasture later or in the morning and you can take a look around at the rest here when you're ready. Let's go into town and get some lunch. The best place is Tilly's. I'll drive."

Sheila liked the offer. So much at one time was so much. She asked Carson, "Sure, where is your car? Are you sure we can't just take mine?"

Carson grinned, "No, girlie, no need for your car, we take the go-cart. It's only a mile. I do it all the time. Come on back out and you two can climb in. Bring the doggies."

The three adults and the two dogs left the house and walked (and padded) out to the golf cart. Cirtron looked with interest at something that was bolted to the back of the cart. It was an aluminum half barrel; meant to hold beer. "Ya, Mon! Ya, take de beer right t'along. Dat be an idea, ah yes, mon."

"Sorry, my curly headed friend, that's not beer. It's a tank for propane gas that one of my buddies made up for me. He attached it to the go-cart and it's got a fuel pipe welded on for the engine and a special valve to fill it. I can go for days with this baby," Carson explained with a little pride. "But don't worry Cirtron, they've got plenty of beer at Tilly's. Just get in. Sheila? You take the doggies and sit in back."

"Ah, mon. Not to be so," Cirtron raised one hand and pointed up with his forefinger and continued. "D'lady, wid de respect mon, she be de one t'sit up in de front, mon."

Sheila was about to intervene but Carson spoke first. "Trust me, let Sheila and the doggies get in back, you and I sit up front and you'll see why."

Sheila said, "Cirtron, go ahead, it's not a problem. Just get in. I'll take the dogs."

Cirtron shrugged, Sheila picked up Redstripe and Paris, each under one arm, climbed in and Carson stepped in and lowered her pudgy frame into the driver's seat. Cirtron took the passenger seat in the front of the golf cart. Before they rolled off, Carson reached under the dash and pulled out two pair of clear safety glasses complete with side protectors. Settling one pair on her own face she handed the other to Cirtron. "Put 'em on. You'll need 'em. We got no windshield on this little buggy."

"My god," said Sheila, "How fast does this thing go?"

Carson answered, "Its not speed, girlie. You'll see."

Taking It to Tilly's

THE LITTLE golf cart, dogs and passengers aboard, beer keg bearing propane on the back, wheeled down the driveway to the road. Near the Fire Identification Number sign, Carson stopped and looked both ways. Seeing things were clear from both directions, she pressed on the accelerator and made the way across the asphalt and unto the gravel shoulder on the opposite side of the road. She turned left and headed south. The moving golf cart began to jostle and shake and Cirtron grabbed the dash with one hand to steady himself. Sheila was not so lucky. She had the dogs each under one arm and no hands left with which to brace herself. Redstripe and Paris began to pant and shake and the sitting end of Sheila began to bounce and slide from one end of the back seat bench to the other. Sheila and the dogs remained attached to her sliding backside but it was a near thing.

"Yeah!" shouted Carson, "Here we go folks! Hang tight!"

Sheila had no comment. She was too busy balancing. The dogs just shook and panted. Cirtron managed a grunt and the unlikely entourage proceeded down the gravel shoulder. Carson leaned over the steering wheel and peered forward. The toothy grin on her face could not be seen by her passengers but would have competed pretty well with the gleeful expression of a fourteen year old on a roller coaster. After only a few hundred yards of gravel shoulder passed under the golf cart wheels, the first semi-trailer passed them. The golf cart rocked as the wind of passage of the semi hit the little vehicle. The sound of the diesel engine and the buffeting air were deafening in the windowless golf cart and the dogs began to bark while Cirtron gripped, Sheila continued to slide and Carson kept grinning. Road dirt and gravel and chunks of this and that flew up from the sixteen wheels of the semi and hit the rocking golf cart like shrapnel. It all bounced up and hit making loud clicks on the side of the cart and then unto the chests and faces of Cirtron and Carson sitting in the front. Sheila and the dogs, still in the back, were spared the onslaught.

The safety glasses Carson had donned and the ones she had given to Cirtron held. Unseen little projectiles bounced against the plastic lenses and fell into the foot wells. Cirtron yelled, "Ah, NO MON, de stone! Watch for de stone, mon!"

Carson just cackled, "Heh, Heh, Heh! I told you it wasn't speed! Cirtron, keep those glasses on. Girlie? You three all okay back there?" She looked over her right shoulder into the back of the golf cart at Sheila and the dogs while letting the golf cart weave dangerously close to a ditch. The cart tilted sharply and Sheila slid hard to the right while hanging on to the hounds and banging her hip.

"We're fine! Watch where you're going! My god!" Sheila yelled.

"Yeah!" shouted Carson, "It won't be far, folks! Hang tight!" Hanging tight was most definitely the order for the day. Redstripe and Paris were not amused.

What is this? the dachshunds were thinking— *that car trip was bad enough but there isn't even a decent place to lie down in here. Dachshunds like us should not have to put up with all of this. Really, this is just not acceptable. We will certainly have something say about this later.*

A car passed. The passengers stared at the golf cart with two dachshunds, the dreadlocked adorned Jamaican and Sheila and the still-grinning Carson. Another semi truck passed, launching more gravel onto and into the cart. The truck driver sounded his air horn, a blast loud enough to rattle the tympanic membranes of humans and hounds. Sheila shouted forward. "What was that!?"

"Just a friend of mine, he pulls a route from Milwaukee to Wautoma every day. His rig carries a load for the big grocery store. Frozen food mostly. That truck has a Thermo King refridge system. Nice guy. Sometimes he drops some overstocks off at my place. Remind me to ask him if he ever has any doggie food. They make some of that stuff you keep in those little pouches. Stays moist like cat food." Carson had been talking again back over her shoulder and the cart wove to the right once more.

"Would you *please* watch where you're going?" Sheila was beginning to tire. Her arms holding the dachshunds were feeling numb. Cirtron, stoic, just hung on to the dash.

"Oh, yeah, not a problem, we're almost there." Carson

The dachshunds had perked up at the mention of food and cats. *Cats? We hate cats. Food is okay, but how much more of all this do we need to put up with? And, by the way, we are dachshunds, not doggies! Let's hear more about those pouches. It's only right.*

After only a mile of travel in the golf cart that had no business running along the side of a busy highway, the crew of the Carson go-cart made it into the town of Wautoma. Carson swung the cart off of the shoulder and onto the paved surface of the main street. A few blocks later, she pulled up and parked the cart just outside Tilly's bar. A broken and crumbling concrete sidewalk led to the entrance for the place and the door looked heavy enough to need two hands to pull it open. Neon signs with beer logos decorated small windows.

"Here we are, folks," announced Carson, "Let's go. I know you all must be hungry."

Sheila, Carson and Cirtron climbed out of the cart. The two dachshunds were placed on the sidewalk, leashes in the hand of Sheila. The hounds had only one thought between them. *Food? There's gotta be. We can smell it.* The dachshund noses had already picked up the odor of French Fries, greasy burgers and all sorts of unhealthy things wafting out and around the edges of the thick door of the bar and grill. Tails began to wag and noses were twitching. The phenomenon was not limited to the hounds. There is nothing like risking one's life in a speeding golf cart to encourage the onset of hunger for any species, be it canine or homo sapiens. The three homo sapiens and the two canines entered the establishment, ready for food and libations.

Tilly's Bar and Grill had been established and owned by a man years past by the name of Attilio "Tilly" Delora. The place had originally catered to the many itinerant workers in the area that came to harvest corn, pickles and peppers in the local fields. Most of that business was now gone, replaced by tourism for folks who came to fish the local lakes in summer and skid across those same lakes in winter on snowmobiles when everything was frozen. Now his granddaughter Sue owned and managed the place as well as the property next door,"Just Rusty's". The two places were nearly as one; a short indoor hallway joined them. Tilly's had a dining room (fish fry on Friday's, chicken on Saturday) with a large, brooding stone fireplace and Just Rusty's had an upstairs electronic archery range that had been installed to bring in business when the local economy began to fall off. The White River, the main water flow feeding the lakes in Wautoma, meandered just behind the two bars. The water passing by ended up in Little Cedar Lake, Irogami Lake and Silver Lake, all mainstays of the local tourism industry. The mainstay of Tilly's Bar and Grill was an oval shaped bar with beer taps scattered here and there. Sue, the owner-manager, greeted Carson and her guests as they pulled back the heavy door and entered the dimness of the bar. "Hey Carson! How are you?"

"Oh, I'm fine, hi Sue," replied Carson while she used her hands to dust off the road grit clinging to her dress. "I just brought in some friends today. Is the kitchen goin'?"

"Yup, ready to go. Hector's cookin' today," answered Sue. "Park yourselves. I'll be right with you."

Lunch at Tilly's

CIRTRON, SHEILA AND CARSON seated themselves on stools at the bar. Carson took Redstripe and Cirtron took Paris. Both dogs planted their back legs in laps and used their front paws to brace up on the bar so they could see the sights. The first thing they saw was a cat. It was stepping arrogantly along the varnished oval surface with a haughty look that only cats can portray. Redstripe and Paris showed interest by making ears go perpendicular to little skulls while lips curled back to show the tips of teeth.

Sheila, the one without a lap dog, asked the bartender. "Uh, Sue? Do I have your name right? What's with the cat? Should we be in here with the dogs?"

Sue laughed. "Don't worry about it. We always have dogs in here. The cat? That's Joe, he's our patrol cat. He just goes in circles around the bar all day and night and picks up scraps. We never have to feed him cat food. Just watch your stuff when I bring it out. He'll snatch it before you can wink. By the way, what are those little guys? Are those like wiener dogs? They're cute. I'll find something for them."

Redstripe and Paris listened and thought, *Things are NOT getting better. Can't that person tell we are ladies and not guys? Really! Besides, that cat needs a good bite.*

Not realizing she was interrupting the dachshunds' thoughts, Carson told Sue, "Get us three cheeseburgers and fries and the usual. Do you have some of that deer sausage for the dogs? They'd like that, I'd bet."

"You got it." Sue wrote an order on a green slip of paper and then fixed up three bloody Marys with beer chasers and placed them in front of Cirtron, Sheila and Carson. "Be right back. I'll take this to Hector. I'll get the wieners some sausage. Hey, get it? Wieners? Sausage? Ha! I can't stand it!" The dogs sniffed at the drinks from their vantage points on Carson's and Cirtron's laps. The spicy smell was not of much interest to them. Both snorted with dog disgust.

Redstripe and Paris continued to watch Joe the cat parade around the bar top. Their little heads moved back and forth, eyes focused on the feline. The cat circled around and the dogs followed its progress with wide eyes and widened nostrils. Swiveling heads in synch, the hounds looked like two slow-motion spectators at a tennis match. Cirtron took a moment to look around as he balanced a hound with one hand and used the other to reach for the spice- and vodka-laced tomato juice on the bar in front of him.

Cirtron saw that the dark stained walls had posters pinned to them. Many were of racing cars and some were of bikini clad young women holding bottles of beer. A pinball machine and some sort of long table strewn with white dust and little bowling pins on one end occupied some of the space not given over to the bar and stools. A music player with a rack of shiny compact disks behind glass sat at the end of the room. Redstripe and Paris were still eye locked on and tracking Joe the cat.

Besides the two dogs, Cirtron, Sheila, Carson and Joe the cat, only two sets of other people were at the bar. Two were men in tee shirts and jeans and baseball caps. Two were senior women whose white hair had turned a little greenish purple from cheap hair treatments. Both pairs were alternately slurping from mugs of beer, using French fries to shovel ketchup out of their red oval plastic basket look-a-likes and biting off chunks of hamburgers. It was slurp, shovel and bite. Place the burger back in the basket and slurp and shovel once more. The gastric-based performance was rhythmic. Joe the cat stopped in front of each pair in turn and was shooed off with the waving of hands each time. The eaters did not even have to look up.

While the eaters ate, the cat patrolled and the dachshund heads swiveled, Carson was talking to Sheila. "You're gonna love these burgers. And the fries are great too. Lots of grease. Anytime I'm feeling a little slow I come in here and it all gets me going right away. There's nothing like a burger at Tilly's to get an old lady's insides moving again, if you know what I mean."

Sheila was dismayed to realize she knew exactly what Carson meant. She began to think of salad.

Breaking the choreography of the slurp, shovel and bite show, one of the men paused and peered across the bar at Cirtron. He reached down and tapped his knuckles on his lunch partner's leg. "Hey! It's Bob Marley! How ya' doin' Bob?" He leaned back a bit on his stool, his partner clapped him on the shoulder and they both began to giggle.

Sheila thought that grown men should never giggle. Carson sipped at her drink. The dog's ears perked up, two sets of fuzzy radars aimed at the source of the new voice. *Now what?* they were thinking, *We can smell food! Let's get on with this.*

All that went through Cirtron's mind was, *"Ah, no. Not again, mon!"*

Sue returned from the kitchen with just two plates. Each had a little pile of sausages cut into thin slices about the diameter of a quarter. She clanked one down each in front of the two hounds. "Eat up guys!" Redstripe and Paris were too interested in the plates to be concerned about another gender insult. Sue turned to the two men. "You two can just shut up. These folks are with Carson here, leave the guy alone and go find your brains somewhere, would you? You wanna a couple more beers? Or do you want Carson mad at you?"

"C'mon Sue, I was just kidding," said the one man. "Ms. Carson, I didn't mean anything. Me and Bobby here were just having fun, okay?"

Carson nodded and sipped more of her drink. The two women with the purple green coiffures whispered to each other. Sue returned to the kitchen. Redstripe and Paris were already licking the remnants of sausage off of their plates. Cirtron looked down, hoping for peace and covering his feelings by adjusting Paris on his lap, her paws still on the bar while she lapped at the sausage plate. The man was not admonished. He returned one more comment. "But, anyway, shouldn't this guy like maybe comb his hair once in a while?"

Sheila looked down, placed both hands flat on the bar and turned her head. "Okay, boys and girls, that's it." Carson placed a hand on her arm but Sheila shook it off and rose to step to the other side of the bar where the two men sat with their unfinished food and greasy napkins. She stopped as the men hiked themselves around to see her.

"I have a question for you," Sheila said, her arms folded across her chest. "Do you have a belt buckle?"

"Well, yeah, I sure do. Did you want to see it?" The man grinned impolitely.

"Sheila explained, "Well, what I really want to do is just borrow it a minute."

"What? For what?"

"I notice you can't hear very well. The bartender told you to leave my friend alone. So could I just borrow that buckle a minute so I can use it to clean out your ears? I'm only trying to help." Sheila stood and smiled. The man's friend covered his mouth with his hand and started to snort the snort of held in check chuckles. The first man lost his grin and looked over at Carson.

"Don't look at me, buddy. The girlie can handle herself it seems to me. Maybe you might want to just be nice?" Carson did not raise her voice at all.

The man rolled his eyes and said, "Yeah, I'm sorry. Hey there guy," he addressed Cirtron across the bar, "We were just kiddin, no harm intended."

"Ya mon, no problem mon, Irie." Cirtron raised a closed fist. "Respect."

Sue came back with the burgers and fries in red plastic baskets and the two dogs and three humans finished lunch at Tilly's in peace. Sheila was really wondering just what place Carson held in this community.

Seeking Supplies

THE THREE humans and the pair of dachshunds left the bar and grill and stepped back to the golf cart. The three of them fitted with two legs clambered in while lifting the dogs up and into the cart. Redstripe and Paris immediately began to pant and shake, anticipating another rough ride. Sheila's thoughts were back in the bar.

"Carson? Who were those two guys? What a couple of wastes of oxygen!"

"Ah, don't worry about it, girlie," Carson answered. "Those are Mike and Bobby. They're harmless. Actually they're sort of friends of mine. They work for Tom's Roofing and replaced the rain gutters on my place for me last year for just the cost of the supplies."

"You mean they did it free? You didn't have to pay them?"

Carson looked straight ahead and said, "Not exactly, we made a trade. I'll explain sometime."

Sheila didn't pursue with more questions after hearing Carson's rather mysterious answer. Cirtron was listening carefully. Carson said brightly, "Tell you what you two. Before we go back, I'm gonna take you over to Copps.

Cirtron spoke up right away. "Cops? No, mon. No need for de cops, mon. Have no done any ting. Why we need de cops, mon?"

Carson laughed. "Heh, heh, heh. No, Cirtron, it's Copps; two p's, and that's a big grocery store here in town. It's just down the road. I expect you need some supplies back at your new place; gotta eat, you know, and so do the doggies."

"Ah, Irie. Yes, mon. Be it okay den, mon."

Redstripe and Paris, hearing the "doggie" name again, began to bark; a duet of protest over the offensive label. Sheila sat back, gripping the dogs in anticipation of another rock and roll ride. Cirtron settled back and Carson pressed on the gas pedal while steering the cart out onto the street and down the way to Copps.

Copps Foods was part of a chain of superstores scattered around the middle and north of the State of Wisconsin. There was nothing remarkable about it, a large building set back from the road behind a parking lot that could hold hundreds of cars. A fast food restaurant and a gas station occupied space in the out lot. The windows were plastered with handwritten signs proclaiming specials on price for everything from beer to smoked hams. Carson pulled right up to the front doors with the cart and stopped it on the concrete apron. "Ok, here we are. Sheila, you come with me, I'll show you where everything is and Cirtron, you stay here with the doggies. We won't be long. Let's go girlie." Before Cirtron could protest and before the hounds could respond to the hateful name once more, Carson had climbed out and was waddling toward the automatic doors with Sheila following obediently.

Inside the store, after directing Sheila to grab a grocery cart, (the kind of which the wheels don't work and cause it to travel in all directions but the chosen one) Carson pointed out the aisles that held fresh fruit, vegetables, bread, meat, eggs and the rest of the things needed to stock a refrigerator. The two women passed the liquor shelves and Sheila eyed some bottles of California wine. Carson grabbed a twelve pack of Blatz beer instead. The food run went well, all in all, the cart was half full, and the checkout lane was the next stop. Outside things were not running quite as smoothly. Cirtron and the dogs had left the cart to stretch. Cirtron was pacing with the dogs on their leashes up and down in front of the store.

Not far from the main doors, the store management had placed a mechanical pony. Electric motors in the base holding it up caused the little horse to rock back and forth while circus music played. The little contrivance was there to amuse children and collect seventy five cents from their parents for a two minute ride. A five year old boy was on it while his mother waited in front of him, her grocery cart loaded and overflowing. Cirtron and the dogs needed to investigate.

As the three of them came up to the pony, mother and child, Redstripe and Paris began to bark. They reared up on their back sides, vertical, and began to paw at the air around the moving hooves of the little horse. The little hounds mimicked two noisy furry brown self powered pogo sticks. It may have been they wanted a ride. It may have been the music hurt their ears. The little boy looked down, delighted and shouted, "Heeee! Puppies! Mommy, puppies!"

Mommy was horrified. She could not decide which presented the greatest danger, the black rasta man or the horrible hounds. "Get these wild animals away from my son! What's the matter with you!" Her head jerked back and forth to first look at Cirtron, then the hounds, then her son and then back at Cirtron. "Get them away!" She grabbed her son from the still rocking horse, plopped him in the back of the grocery cart and made a hasty retreat to the parking lot. She called back over her shoulder, "Something should be done about people like you!"

"Puppies!" shouted the little boy.

Cirtron did not know what to say. He reached down to pet Redstripe and Paris. "Not to worry, my small friends. De people, many are without de respect mon."

The dogs, subdued after the woman's outburst thought, *Wild animals? Us? We just wanted to play! Besides, we didn't bite anybody or knock anybody over or anything. There was some good food in that cart, though.*

Cirtron straightened, sighed and wondered if he was going to get used to this new town. The little horse continued to rock as Sheila and Carson came out through the doors to see Cirtron with the two dogs still standing near the little mechanical horse. "Cirtron?" asked Carson. "Aren't you a little big for that?"

"Yes, mon. Ah, no, mon. See, de woman, she not have de respect for de little dogs."

"What woman?" asked Sheila.

"Ah, not to mind, m'lady. Be it okay. Irie. Now we can go, mon?"

"Yup," replied Carson. "Let's dump these bags in the cart and blow this popcorn joint. It's about time we got back. I'll show you the rest of the farm."

Where the Deer and the Antelope Play

THE GOLF CART ride back was not much better than the ride into town. Gravel flew. Winds stirred by passing trucks rocked the little vehicle and all hung on as best they could. Carson whooped and grinned, an aging pilot leaning over the controls of an old biplane. A long silk scarf wrapped around her neck would have completed the picture. Sheila collected another hip bruise and Cirtron's collection of road dirt grew. The dogs shook and panted.

Back at the Armstead farm and after the groceries were stuffed into the fridge and into cupboards, Sheila asked Carson, "So, can you show us the herd? I promised Redstripe and Paris they would get to see some cows."

Cows? Where's the cows? Can we chase them? Dachshund ears perked up.

"Cows?" asked Carson.

"Yes, you know, like 'moo.' Cows," said Sheila. "Where are they?"

"Cows, huh? Well ok, better come with me out back." Carson led the way out the rear door.

Behind the farmhouse, a tract of nearly eight acres spread out covered with some sort of grass, muddy areas and two double acre sections enclosed by heavy duty fencing. The fence posts were nearly six feet high, made of eight by eight inch beams and connected by heavy wire mesh. Piles of baled hay were placed in spots here and there just outside the enclosures and a couple of water troughs could be seen along the inside edges of the fencing. More than a good dozen animals milled about in one of the fenced areas. Grass and hay stuck out from their mouths as they chewed.

Sheila froze. Cirtron put one hand to his beard. Carson began to chuckle. The dogs stood still, pointed and their hackles rose in strips down their backs.

"Oh . . . my . . . god. They're buffaloes!" Sheila could barely get the words out.

"Bison." Carson corrected. "This is a bison ranch. I expect you didn't know?"

"Bison," said Sheila. It wasn't even a question.

"Ah, ya, mon," said Cirtron. "Day look like no cows I have been to see. Lot's of hair, mon. Like mine."

Indeed the high shoulders that sloped down to the lower and smaller hindquarters of the bison were covered with thick mats of hair, not unlike Cirtron's dreadlocks and tangled beard The two dogs began the backward dachshund dance. They each lifted their little heads, let go one bark, took a step back and then barked and stepped again. They'd reversed about three dog lengths before Sheila asked, "What in the world do you do with buffalo—bison I mean?"

Carson was enjoying the surprise of the situation and answered, "Oh, 'bout the same as with cows. You feed them and water them and in the end you can eat them and wear them. They bring a good price if they are cared for well."

Sheila had not recovered. "Oh . . . my . . . god. Bison." And then she thought about the dogs. "Cirtron, grab Redstripe and Paris. I don't want them running under that fence."

"Ya, mon." Sheila should not have worried. The hounds were still dancing backward.

"Good idea," remarked Carson. "Those dogs are already long enough, we don't want them flat too. What do you say we go back into the house, open some of that beer we brought back, and I'll explain some of this?"

"Ya, mon."

"Lead on, Carson, I can't wait to hear."

Inside, the humans sat at the kitchen table with the twelve pack of Blatz torn open in front of them. The dogs scampered into the front room, hopped up onto a worn couch, placed their heads on paws and began to snooze. Carson began her lecture.

"First of all," started Carson, "you might remember I brought over some papers for you. They're over there on the counter top. The bank books, check books, deeds, tax records and all the things related to this property are in there. There should be a survey in there too and a list of all the contacts for things related to the bison like feed suppliers and the processing plant and all of that. I know there's a ledger book with all the expenses as well and the records are pretty good. Actually, while I was taking care of the place, the last entries are mine. I ended up with all the papers when old Armstead's son finally left."

Sheila asked, "This son, I guess he would be my cousin, did he give you all that?"

"No, he didn't. I needed it all to take care of things so I got it from one of the suits at the Midland Bank. Tom Pederson; nice guy but a little old for me. I don't why he's still working. He should be in a rocking chair."

"He just gave it to you? Should he have done that?"

"Well, girlie," answered Carson, "If I was gonna take care of this place for a while, I needed to pay the bills and such. I suppose Tom broke a little rule or two, but he was just being nice. Besides, we made a trade."

"A trade?" asked Sheila. This was the second time she'd heard about trading.

"Ah, mon. What did you make wid de trade, mon?"

Carson gave the same answer as before."I'll explain later. Let me tell you about bison. You really need to know this stuff."

"Now then, you two. There is some stuff you really need to understand. Just let me jabber on a bit and try not to interrupt. Bison are creatures that deserve a great deal of respect. They're sort of the ghosts of a lost culture. But they will take care of your needs over time if you take care of them. They will provide you with a livelihood. This thing is really a partnership between you and them and that partnership between the bison and people goes back a very, very long way. It is one of the great sinful tragedies in time that people did not honor that relationship so well in the past centuries."

Sheila and Cirtron were riveted. Sheila realized they were about to receive a philosophical history lesson and was trying to revamp her impression of this chubby little neighbor, the pilot of golf carts and caretaker of the farm. Cirtron settled back with his Blatz beer and prepared to just listen. Patience was one of Cirtron's better virtues.

Carson continued."Round about two or three hundred years ago, there were tons of these creatures stomping around on the western plains of the United States and Canada. They were the biggest creatures around and few predators messed with them very much except for the young and the sick. I've heard that there were somewhere between thirty and seventy million bison milling about, mostly west of the Mississippi river. I don't suppose they had any white shirted accountants out there counting bison on their handheld computers back then, but most accounts tell of so many bison that herds of them could be seen to stretch clear to the horizon."

Sheila was startled, stared at Carson and said,"Seventy *million?*"

"Don't interrupt. You see, these big hairy critters were the main thing needed by most of the plains Indians out there in the west before our ancestors went out to settle it. Tribes like the Sioux and the Dakotas and lots of others depended on the bison for their lives and their societies. This is where the respect thing comes in. The Native American folks used the bison for clothing, tools, weapons, shelter, food and everything else. They ate the meat, dried some for later, took the hides for shelter, blankets and clothes, and carved up the bones for all kinds of things. They even munched the innards and used the left overs to make things. Of course being dismantled into all these parts was rather tough on the bison. But the native people had great respect for life and realized they were taking a bison life in order to keep their own selves alive. They were in the habit of thanking every bison that was killed for letting them live another day. And they didn't waste anything. That's not like today's folks. Just check the trash anywhere."

"Ya, mon. Respect. I know how dis be true and must be for all de tings under Ga."

Carson looked at Cirtron and smiled. "Yeah, Cirtron, I've heard you use that word; respect. Good for you. But let me keep going here before I forget something. Old ladies don't always think so well."

"I'm beginning to get the impression you think pretty well, Carson," said Sheila.

"Don't interrupt. Now, where was I? Oh yeah, trash. See, there was a time when the people trying to settle this country out in the west did not do so well by the bison. By the end of the eighteen hundreds, most of animals had been killed. There were only a few thousand left and the original millions all died for the wrong reason. In a manner of speaking, the white people wasted them. The bison were killed by the thousands by hunters, the army, explorers and folks that were just heading west. It got so bad that when the railroads went through, people paid to ride the rails and just shoot the bison through the open windows of the trains. The worst part was most of the animals were killed just for their horns or hides or the pure sport of things and the carcasses were left to rot. The bison were all gone after a while and their deaths went for nothing."

"Now then, not only did the bison lose out, but the Native Americans lost big time. In spite of what you might read about the soldiers and the settlers, it wasn't really them that did in the Indians and other native people. It was really the lack of the bison herds that destroyed those cultures. The source for food and shelter and clothing and all that just was gone; wasted by stupidity." Carson reached for and raised a beer can to her lips and gulped. She wiped her mouth with the back of her hand and said, "You can interrupt now."

"De people, day had no respect, mon?"

Sheila was silent.

Carson clunked her beer can back on the table. "So, okay. Here's the deal. Bison are not cows. Sorry you are disappointed not to have any here. But these bison beasts are not to be ignored. Did you see those fences? They're better than six feet high. A full sized bison can jump one up to four feet. They can hit forty miles an hour on a dead run without a lead more than ten or twenty yards and they are big. Most of the time they just stand around and chew but when they get into a mood, they're dangerous. Don't go out there and think you're gonna pet them or rub their noses or something. But if you feed them and water them, that's about all they need and maybe some corn before they go for processing, they'll provide you with a living. They don't even need a barn in winter. The snow just builds up on their backs. Let me tell you, a snow fall on a bison herd looks like something from a Currier and Ives print; very pretty. But you need to understand the respect thing. You have to understand they are the ghosts of a lost culture."

"It's a funny thing. People in this country and in Canada are bringing the bison back. There's herds in some parks out west and there are ranches all over. Last I heard Wisconsin had about seven thousand bison residents. What's funny is that it's the descendants of the people who wiped out most of the bison hundreds of years ago who are trying to bring them back. Odd, hey? A bunch of organizations have sprung up here and there that have people as members who try to promote the bison and bison ranching. In fact, because bison don't have a history of folks messing with their breeding and health and meat production and all that over time like with cows, the animals are pretty healthy and don't need much in the way of veterinary attention. No antibiotics or hormones or that stuff. They do just fine on their own."

Carson finally wound down and Sheila asked,"So, let me see if we have this straight. We raise the bison, and then send them off to some processing plant? Sell them for the meat and hides?"

"Yup," nodded Carson,"just so that you have some respect for them. That's my whole point."

Cirtron was quiet, sipping beer and thinking but Sheila had another question."Um, how do we get more bison? I mean, I noticed all the animals inside the fences had horns. Don't we need some girl bisons? I mean, well, you know?"

Carson looked up at the ceiling and started laughing. Her stocky body shook as she tapered off into a snicker and then took a breath and said,"Oh! I'm sorry! I forgot! There is one bull out there. You'll get calves when the time is right. Usually 'round April."

Sheila did not get it,"But . . ."

"Girlie..Sheila, with bison, both the males and the females have horns. You gotta look down, not up, to tell who's who."

Cirtron spoke. "De lady bison have de horns, mon?"

Carson, snickering again, opened her eyes wide and said solemnly to Cirtron, "Well, yes, my dark friend. After all, don't lady people get horns sometimes?"

The rasta man opened his mouth to ask another question but Sheila got the pun and said, "Forget it, Cirtron, Carson is joking. Don't go there."

"Where would I go? I not be going t'anywhere."

Sheila was getting too tired to try to explain and Carson just smiled and said, "Tell you what, you two, let's have another beer and then I'm off to my place. I'll leave you alone and you can get some rest. God knows these old bones of mine need some too. I'll come see you tomorrow and show you where more things are out in the shed. If that's alright?"

"Sounds good. And thank you, by the way. I don't think I said that," replied Sheila.

"Irie," said Cirtron.

Beer tabs clicked, they drank and Sheila excused herself to walk the dogs, on leashes this time, out in the front. Dachshund noses were more interested in sniffing the evening air than in taking care of business, but things did get done and Redstripe, Paris and their mistress returned to the farmhouse. Inside, her second beer can empty, Carson said good night and left by the main door. Sheila and Cirtron could soon hear the hum of the golf cart fading as it followed the path to the old lady's place next door.

Thunder in the Grass

ON THE FIRST morning that Sheila and Cirtron and the dogs rose from sleep in their new home, Sheila cooked breakfast. "Don't expect this will become a habit," she said to Cirtron. "I'm no morning cook and I don't get up early if I don't have to."

"No problem, mon," Cirtron answered. He studied the burnt toast and runny eggs on his plate. "I can cook d'next time. 'Like t'do so."

"Fair enough. Look, I'm going to go take a shower and then we can go out and check on the bison. Feed the ladies, would you?" Cirtron nodded and when Sheila left he scraped his breakfast in two portions into the dog dishes. Redstripe and Paris were very appreciative; dachshunds *never* waste people food and the sounds of slurps and dachshund grunts and the banging of dog bowls filled the kitchen. Under the circumstances, the two dogs were hoping that Sheila would cook breakfast often.

With breakfast finished, the hounds sated and Sheila cleaned up, it was time for the four new resident ranchers to go out back and meet the bison. Cirtron splashed some water from the kitchen faucet on his face, dried with a dish towel and Sheila, down from the upstairs bath, opened the rear door. The hounds darted out before either of the two humans had even set a foot over the threshold. Redstripe and Paris, a matched pair of furry brown blurs, catapulted themselves at grass-top level straight across the lawn separating the house from the pasture. The two stopped at the fence, noses extended through the wire mesh. Both were busy inhaling bison smells and stood rigid, aimed at the big animals. Dachshund chests were pumping like little bellows to power their snouts and Redstripe and Paris were ready for trouble. Trouble there would be. It usually comes when dachshunds are in the picture. Sheila and Cirtron caught up to the dogs.

"Cirtron! Grab the dogs!"

"No, problem, mon. Not t'get true de fence, mon. Irie."

"Well," said Sheila, "maybe. But I don't want them in there. They'll get hurt or flattened. Cirtron, you know the ladies. They'll go anywhere. Silly things."

"Ya, mon. Silly. Hah! Day ha' none of d'sense. Maybe put dem 'pon de leash?"

Sheila, worried, tried to think reasonably, "No, let's just see what they do. I think you're right. It would be tough for them to get through that wire fence. They wouldn't like to be tied so let's just keep an eye on them, ok? Redstripe! Paris! Get away from that fence! Those things in there would as soon stomp you as look at you!"

The dachshunds were not interested in advice and remained at the fence; long low bodies on the outside with noses sticking through to the inside. The smells could not be ignored and twin tails twitched in tandem. The dogs began to wuff and whine. *Bison! How cool is that?* they were thinking.

Sheila had her own thoughts. "Cirtron, what do we do here, do we feed them or what?"

"I tin we do de feed, mon, not d'what. Seems dere be de hay on de sides for de beasts, water in is de tanks, so we need t'trow it over de fence where d'beasts kin eat it, yes?"

"Sounds right to me, let's go lift some bales I guess. That fence looks pretty high to be tossing over, but we can try. I wonder were Carson is? She said she'd be over. Maybe she has a better idea. I suspect she does."

"Ya, mon. Be it for now we toss, yes?"

Cirtron and Sheila made their way around the to the first pile of hay bales while Redstripe and Paris found a way to scramble under the fence and into the bison pasture.

The first pile of hay reached nearly to the top of the fence. Sheila and Cirtron climbed up on the stack and pushed the first couple of rectangular compacted bales over the fence and into the pasture. Some of the bison looked over and made their way to the forage. Sheila and Cirtron pushed four more bales over and in but the pile was getting lower and the bales were so heavy that the next was going to be a problem to lift and toss. Both of them were beginning to sweat from the effort. Three bison arrived to chew at the fresh chunks of hay. They began to eat the stuff, restraining twine and all.

Redstripe and Paris had moseyed across the pasture, moving slower and more cautiously than on the run from the house, and began to bark and howl and snort and do the backward dachshund dance at the first bison they came near. The big hairy bovine, the subject of their attention, was not amused. She turned her huge head sideways to get a look at the two little irritating canines and bellowed. Bison are herd animals. They seek protection as a group. While Redstripe and Paris were barking at the single bison the bellowing summoned her friends. They came quickly. And the weight on their hooves shook the ground in their haste to come to the support of their herd mate. The two humans on top the hale bales could feel the thumping of the bison through the ground and even up through the pile on which they were perched. Both of them look up, concerned.

Sheila spotted the dachshunds and screamed. The bison gathered in a tight group to confront the dogs. The bovine heads were lowered. They were not happy. Redstripe and Paris continued to slowly back but they did not know whether to stand their ground or run. *This was not in the plans,* they thought. Sheila was in a panic. "Cirtron! The dogs! Get the dogs!"

Cirtron did not hesitate. He leaped off the pile of hay bales and over the fence landing hard after the six foot drop and dropping to his knees. He recovered quickly and headed for the hounds but the first bison beat him in the race. She lowered her head even further, stomped forward toward the hounds and used her nose to give Paris a little push. Paris weighed in at about ten pounds. The bison tipped the scales at about a half ton. The bison won simply by the laws of physics and Paris was rolled over and over in the grass, a hair-covered tootsie roll without a wrapper. Redstripe figured this was time to exit and headed toward the edge of the pasture where Sheila was still screaming and waving her arms. Cirtron got to Paris and bent down to grab her, ignoring the bison.

"No! No! You dog, not to worry at the hairy cows, they will . . ."

It was too late. The bison, still aggravated, bumped Cirtron with his dachshund burden and sent both of them down and into the mud and grass of the pasture. Bison manure is supposed to be rather clean but some of it coated Cirtron and Paris as they lay there trying to catch their breath. The bison stopped. Perhaps it had had enough fun for the moment but it remained hovering a few feet away. The rest of the herd just stood by.

"Cirtron! GET OUT OF THERE!" Sheila had gone over the fence to retrieve Redstripe and was trying to climb back out to safety. "Cirtron! Get up! Get out of there!"

"Ya, mon," said Cirtron from his place in the mud and manure. "Be right dere, mon." He got up and made his way quickly to the fence, handed over Paris and climbed up and over to the pile of bales. "Maybe d'fence, n'work so well?"

Sheila did not answer at first, she only was checking on the two hounds. She found them sound and then turned to Cirtron. "You stink. And so do the dogs. What a mess."

"Ya, mon. De smell. But de dogs, day be okay. Irie."

Sheila immediately felt bad. "Oh, Cirtron, I'm sorry! I was so worried and scared. You saved Redstripe and Paris! How can I thank you?"

"Ah, no problem, mon, m'lady. I just go to wash. But now, maybe put d'dogs 'pon de leash?"

"Yes, mon," smiled Sheila. "I promise."

The hum of the golf cart slithered into Sheila's and Cirtron's awareness. They looked over to see Carson in the cart around the corner of the pasture. Even from a ways away, Carson could see that things were a bit amiss and that Cirtron and Paris were filthy.

"Hey! Good morning!" she shouted, "I told you not to try to pet the bison, didn't I?"

"We'll meet you in the kitchen," shouted Sheila. We've got some cleaning up to do and we have some questions about this hay."

Carson waved and turned the golf cart toward the house.

Cirtron and Sheila, each with a dog under an arm, made their way back to the house. Carson was already waiting in the kitchen. "My god, man," she said to Cirtron, "You really stink! Paris, is that Paris under all that goo? She won't get prizes for cleanliness either."

"Ya, mon. We go up for de bath. Irie."

While Carson and Sheila seated themselves at the table in the kitchen, Cirtron went up the stairs and to the bathtub. He filled it, undressed and plunked himself in right along with the two dogs. While Paris was the one that really needed the bath, he figured that it would do no harm to dunk Redstripe too. Once the three of them were soaped and scrubbed, the water looked pretty bad but most of the bison smells left down the drain. Afterward, two wet and indignant dachshunds shook themselves dry and scattered water all over the floor and walls. Cirtron dried off with a towel.

Redstripe and Paris were thinking, *What was that BATH all about? We hate water! And actually if anyone would have cared to ask us, we LIKED those smells.*

Cirtron looked down and said to them,"No more under de fence. Not safe for d'little dogs, ah?"

Redstripe and Paris, still miffed, just turned and left the bathroom. They gallumped down the stairs and climbed on a couch in the front room to pout for a while. The Jamaican just sighed, dressed and went down to join the women in the kitchen. He entered the room as Carson was talking.

" . . . so you see there's no reason to try to lift all that hay over the top. Oh, Cirtron! You're clean. Good. I was telling Sheila about the little bobcat machine in the shed. I'm sure the two of you can figure how to work it. It's got a set of spiney things on the front and you can use it to lift the bales over the fence and drop them in. You don't have to work so hard with the hay.

"Speaking of hay, now that the next crop has been cut, the feed company will deliver the big bales and dump them in the pasture in a day or so. I don't know if you've seen those things in the fields around here, they're big and round and better than six feet across. They've got these machines that cut and then roll the stuff into these huge wheels. That'll last the bison for a while and you can just watch and order more when you need it. You'll pay for it, of course. But then all you need to do is make sure the water troughs are full, there's a pump in the shed that pushes the water through underground pipes. You just make sure it always has power out there. Ok?"

"Ya, mon. I understand de ting."

Sheila said it sounded simple even though she had some doubts about lots of things after living through the last couple of days. As she spoke, two of the objects of her most serious concerns trotted into the kitchen. They approached the table and each gave a little bark.

"Cirtron?" asked Sheila, "You did feed them, didn't you?"

Cirtron answered, "Ya, mon. Day finished while you were in d'shower." He was hoping Sheila would not ask *what* they were fed. Dachshund meal times basically coincide with all of their waking hours so the two dogs stayed to pester down under the kitchen table. Carson grinned down at them and told them to be still.

The old lady began again, "Now then, the dogs. We can't have them crawling under that fence, although god knows how they did it, and hurting themselves or disturbing the herd. You're gonna have to do something about that and . . ."

Sheila interjected, "I know, I know. I just hate to see them tied. What do we do, build a big fence just for them?"

"Girlie, you've got to do something about that interrupting habit of yours. Let me finish. I think I know what you can do. Just listen."

Admonished, Sheila fell silent and sat back but she was wondering precisely who was supposed to running this place. She knew she needed Carson's help, but the woman was so commandeering. Cirtron, being Cirtron, knew when to be quiet and he did so. He was thinking more of what fun it might be to drive that bobcat around. Under the table, the two hounds sensed they were the subject of the conversation and went quiet. Ears were perked. Tails were still.

Carson continued."Building a new fence would not be a bad idea. But I have a better one. What you need to do is install fencing on the *outside* of the pasture fencing. You need strong stuff with small openings in the mesh. Tack it on about three feet up and that should do it. But there is a trick. You see you need to dig that new fencing down into the ground. I'd say another two feet down should work and then the dogs can't dig under it. It's the same way we protect gardens so the rabbits and such can't in around here. The trick is to get that fencing deep in the ground where nothing can dig under. In this case, your doggies. Actually, some people dig a three foot trough and fill it with concrete and stick the fencing down into that. But this should work and the concrete is expensive. This isn't a set of vegetable gardens; this is a big area." Carson stopped and leaned back, smiling, proud of herself and her idea.

"Ya, mon. Lot's of work and maybe d'money too?"

Sheila broke her silence and said, "It doesn't matter. We have to do this. This morning was way too close for my nerves and if it isn't the dachshunds that get hurt, it will one of us chasing them like fools through a stampede. I can pay what is needed."

Carson had still another answer. "In this case, you don't have to worry. I happen to have a friend who installs fencing, has the materials and tools to do this quickly, and not charge a thing."

"What?" exclaimed Sheila. Cirtron was coolly interested and did not speak.

"Well, I can work it out. See, it just so happens this fencing friend is ready for a trade."

Trader Carson

SHEILA AND CIRTRON had been hearing about this trading business for two days. This time Sheila was determined to press for an answer from Carson even though the woman had demurred several times before when asked. "Carson," demanded Sheila, "what is all this trading business? I've asked you two or three times and you said you'd explain later. I think it is later now, don't you?"

Carson exhaled slowly. "Yeah, I suppose you're right. But I think it is easier to show you than tell you. We need to take a little trip out the back of my place. Let's go climb in my go-cart and I'll take you there. You can take the doggies if you want."

"Fine. And they're dachshunds, not doggies." Sheila's impatience was beginning to bubble just a bit.

Carson shrugged, "Fine yourself, girlie, and bring the dachshunds. But leash 'em and don't let 'em loose. Come on then, you too, Cirtron, I think you'll like this."

The four left the house and boarded the little golf cart for another ride. Sheila sat in front this time and Cirtron took the back with the two hounds. Redstripe and Paris were ready for another adventure; noses sniffing and tails wagging. Undaunted that they'd nearly become bison stepping stones, they were hoping for more fun. *More cats? More of those hairy cows? Food? What's next?* Jaws opened, tongues dangled out, and they began to pant.

Carson drove the golf cart over the track that led between the two properties and then around the back of her house. Another worn, double-rutted path ran from the rear of her home and out to what was nearly two acres of corn growing in neat rows. The plants were not quite three feet tall, had not produced their distinctive silklike tassels yet, but they looked healthy and deeply green. Carson took the four of them out over the little path and pulled up just a few feet away from the field of corn. "Ok, you guys," directed Carson, "climb out and have a look."

"What are we looking at?" Sheila was confused. "It's just a bunch of corn for pete's sake. What do we do, build a fence out of corn stalks?" Sheila just stood there, staring at the corn rows wondering what nonsense she would hear next.

Carson took Sheila gently by one elbow. She said, in an uncharacteristically soft voice, "Honey, look closer, look between the rows. It's not the corn we came out here to see. Cirtron? You look too, you'll see it, I'm sure."

Sheila took a couple of steps forward and aimed her gaze between one the rows. Where she expected to see dirt, the lanes between the stalks seemed crowded with weeds. Cirtron took a closer look and just froze, his lower jaw dropped, threatening to take permanent residence, whiskers and all, in the middle of this chest.

Sheila said, "Yeah? So what? Somebody needs to get out here with a hoe or something. Or one of those machines that the farmers all have. Aren't you supposed to keep the rows clean of weeds so the corn grows better? What a mess!"

Cirtron broke out of his stupor, closed his mouth and began to grin. Before he could say anything he dropped with a hard sounding plop on the edge of the field, sitting with his elbows on his knees and his head in his hands. Sheila was alarmed. "Cirtron, are you alright? What's wrong? Did you get hurt out with those bison?" She was frightened and then maddened because Cirtron began to laugh.

Cirtron sat there, head in hands with chuckles coming out from the back of his throat, a hoarse sound, almost as if he was coughing. He raised his head, looked up and let go a loud peal of pure laughter that set the hounds to barking. Carson was trying to hold back giggles and that made Sheila even madder. She turned to the giggling old woman and shouted, "What is going on here?! What is so damn funny?!"

Carson continued to try to suppress her laughter, only squeaks and giggles escaping and said nothing. Her hand was clamped over her mouth. Cirtron rolled onto his side; still laughing so hard his breathing was coming into question. Redstripe and Paris barked and added to the din. Sheila looked again at the weeds, saw Cirtron laughing in the grass, glanced at Carson and some switch clicked closed in her brain.

"Oh . . . my . . . god!" Once more, she could hardly get words out. "Carson! *This* is what you trade with!"

Carson took a deep breath, calmed herself and said, "Yup, the corn isn't the real crop. The weeds are. You sort of couldn't see the forest for the trees, girlie, but I figured Cirtron would, him being from Jamaica and all that."

Sheila looked at the weeds, the corn, the old fat and dumpy woman who drove a golf cart and began to feel dizzy. She just could not grasp this, on top of the bison, and get it all into one coherent picture she could understand.

Carson saw this and said, "Tell you what, let's go back to my place and I will explain all this. It really is not that complicated. It's okay. Really. Come on, bring the dachshunds."

Sheila glanced over to where Cirtron had been laying and was about to tell him to get into the golf cart, but he was not there. She turned to the cornfield and saw him a few rows over, bent down, pulling at weeds and stuffing his pockets. "Dammit, Cirtron! Get out of there!"

"Sheila?" Carson said sternly. "Don't worry. He's welcome. There's plenty."

Cirtron, Sheila, Carson and the two dogs finally climbed back into the golf cart. In the back, Redstripe and Paris sniffed at Cirtron's pockets and then snorted and looked away. They were not interested. The little cart hummed its way back down the rutted path and then the five of them entered Carson's house. Sheila was completely distracted by what she had seen but did have a moment of clarity to look around inside. The place was obsessively neat with no clutter and the kitchen was immaculate. Carson noticed Sheila's glances and said, "Hey, you know? When you live alone, you have plenty of time for cleaning. Go make yourselves comfortable in the living room. I'll get some coffee." She pointed. "Its right through there." Sheila, Cirtron and the hounds made themselves comfortable on brocaded furniture with carved wooden legs kept company by end tables topped with doilies. The room was open through several windows to the morning light and everything was bright and smelled fresh. Anyone's grandmother could have occupied the place. Sheila's head was still spinning; the dogs had climbed into Cirtron's lap for a morning snooze. Cirtron absently patted his pockets. Carson came in with three mugs on a tray. The coffee was spiked with anise seed.

Carson seated herself and started talking after the mugs were handed around.

"Now then, first off, I suppose *you're* wondering: I don't use the stuff. Not much anyway unless my arthritis is kicking up. I use it to trade for things I need. Mr. Carson did not leave me much in the way of insurance or a pension and our dear government does not give me enough of that social security stuff to keep up the place. So I trade for the shortfalls like the roof and maintenance and all that. You'll get that dachshund deterrent fencing out of it. Fall is not that far away and most years I have the boys plow most of what is not used under anyway. Drives 'em nuts. Sheila, are you going to interrupt?"

Sheila just waved a hand and then put a finger to her lips. She was listening.

Carson said, "Good." And then continued.

"Here is how it all works. You should realize my grandfather was a judge in this county. My family, most of them gone now, all got to know all the politicians and the law folks and such, most just through social connections, but the ties stayed in place. You would be surprised about all the people in high places around this area that know me and I trade with. There's lawyers and bankers and county people and even people that work in good old Washington of the D and C. By the way I use that way of naming our capitol for a reason. Figure it out. Wanna interrupt, Sheila?"

"No."

"Good enough. So I trade with them all. But I never take money. Only service and materials like for your fencing. And those that are not one of the big folks are related or have made themselves useful with their votes or some such thing or another and they have nothing to fear if they get involved with a trade with me. They are all pretty much protected unless they get stupid and try to sell some stuff elsewhere, not for their own use. That has happened now and then and the results are always pretty sad. For me, I just have to make the field look nice, cosmetic I guess, so no one gets embarrassed. That's why the corn is there."

"I told you I made a trade to get the bank things for your uncle. That worked because the banker Tom Pederson's wife is suffering terribly from some sort of muscle disease. I don't understand it but I do know she would have put herself into her own grave a while back without my trading. The guy who is going to do your fencing is just trying to get his business going a little stronger. He will be able to say he did the work on the Armstead Ranch and use that to promote things. Besides, he'll have to do the work on a weekend and that will keep him out of Tilly's and his wife will be pleased. I think she uses a little of the trade herself. The fellows who did my roof and gutters still had to buy the supplies for the job. They paid for those and one of the local suppliers got the sale, See? I am really an underground community service. I add to the economy."

Carson paused so Sheila asked, "Don't you worry about that stuff out there in the back?"

"No. I don't. See, the people that trade with me are all over the county. I am pretty much the only game in town, so to speak, and I am honest and generous. I don't talk when I don't need to. If someone would go out there and steal, the rest of the traders would sort of take care of things if you know what I mean. I do worry that some animals get in there and get sick but you may have noticed that your doggies, the dachshunds, sorry, just turned up their noses. I don't worry too much. But one time, as a matter of fact, when old Armstead was moving the bison from one pasture to another, one of the bison got loose and wandered into the cornfield. It ate down a whole row of corn and munched up the weeds at the same time. Boy, I gotta tell you, that bison got such a case of loose stools it was dangerous. The stuff that was coming out beneath the tail of that beast was so strong and furious the stream could have knocked a cat off a fence post from six feet away. The animal got better but old Armstead was not too happy. I just told him to watch his gates."

During Carson's lecture, the dachshunds had become restless. Cirtron handed each down to the floor and they ambled over to Carson where she was seated in her chair. They pawed at her legs and Carson leaned down, grabbed each one in turn and placed them in her own lap. "I could get used to these little . . . what do you call them, ladies? They're cute." Then she settled back with the dachshunds in her lap and closed her eyes.

Sheila looked over at Cirtron. "I think she fell asleep. What should we do?"

"Ah, we go back to t'other house. Leave d'little dogs with her. Come back later and let dem all sleep a while. She be d'good lady, I tink."

"I suppose that's okay," Sheila was still in a state of slight disorientation. "I suppose you just want to go back and play with that bobcat, huh?"

"Ya, mon. Dat too."

The Wautoma Flute

TWO MONTHS went by and life for Sheila, Cirtron and the hounds, with the help and support of Carson, settled into routine. Carson had "traded" for the extra fencing and there were no more bison-dachshund confrontations. Huge bales of hay in rolls had been delivered to pasture while Cirtron continued to move the smaller bales around with the bobcat. He always found an excuse to drive it out to the pastures if for no other reason than to just check on things. Redstripe and Paris were pretty much free to just wander about and sniff the grass and chase the fall butterflies or to make an occasional visit for shaking and smelling at the edge of the fencing for the bison. More evenings than not, the three humans shared dinner at one house or the other while the dachshunds begged scraps. With the group dinners and table scraps, the smelly old bison, the ability to wander about freely and the abundant gophers, the hounds found themselves in their own version of dachshund heaven; an endless vista of freedom, smells, fun and food.

One typical afternoon, the two dachshunds were lying in the shade of the back of the house, recovering from an almost-successful gopher hunt. They were tired. But a half hour snooze brought Redstripe up and into alert mode. She nosed Paris who was still sleeping with half closed eyes. *Paris, wake up! I see butterflies!* Paris stirred. *Go chase them yourself, I'm busy.* Paris went back to sleep. Redstripe wandered off to harass butterflies.

Carson had taken Cirtron into town on supply runs on many occasions and one of the first ones was to the "Coast to Coast Do-It-

Best" hardware store. Sheila had directed Cirtron to buy some paint and cleaning things for the inside of the old farm house. Carson parked the golf cart outside the hardware store and told Cirtron she would wait for him.

The rasta man entered the store and approached the check out counter. "Ya, mon. I need d'paint and d'brushes and d'tings ta clean d'walls, mon." He'd addressed two men standing behind the counter. Each had a shirt with a name stitched above the pocket; one label read Kelly and one read Robert. Robert turned to Kelly.

"Go help this gentleman out. He needs paint and maybe some ammonia and maybe a box of Borax. Don't forget a paint tray and the brushes. Get him a bucket, too. And a scrub brush."

Kelly seemed affronted. "Why do I have to go? Are your feet painted on?"

The two men glared at each other. Cirtron held up a hand and said, "Ah, no need to have d'arguing. Jus tell me where t'go in d'store?"

Robert looked away from Kelly and then at Cirtron. "Oh, don't worry about it. We were just giving each other a hard time. It passes the day. We've had this store for nearly forty years and we need to have a little fun now and then. Here, come with me, we'll find your stuff." Robert led Cirtron toward the back of the store down and between rows of shelves crowded with nuts, bolts, tools, endless widgets and garden supplies and most things seen under the sun. He stopped at a row of shelves with cans of paint; a floor mounted mixer was bolted down nearby. "What color?"

"I tink d'white, she be okay."

"We've got clamshell white, eggshell white, frost white and, let me see, yes, we have glacier white and I believe some storm cloud white. What will it be?"

"No need for de clams or de eggs mon, just need d'white. Do ya' have d'white?"

Robert smiled. "Yup, it's called white. Let me grab two cans and then I don't have to mix nothin', just give you the base. You can always come back for more and we won't have to worry about matching it."

Cirtron said thank you. Robert led him out to the front and pointed to the other supplies for the rasta man. The pile of purchases was placed on the counter and Kelly rang it all up. Once the paint and supplies were bagged, both Kelly and Robert helped carry the things out to the golf cart and the waiting Carson. Kelly raised a hand. "'Lo, Ms. Carson, have a good day, hey?"

"I'll see what I can do with it, Kelly. You too."

Carson started the golf cart, Cirtron, paint and supplies on board, and headed back to the farm. Cirtron was thinking that he had not been insulted or teased even once. Kelly and Robert were nice guys.

The rest of that day, Cirtron spent his time cleaning the walls of the front room at the old farmhouse and painting with the white, not eggshell, not clamshell, not frost, just plain white. Redstripe and Paris naturally wanted to help and made sure they each had noses half covered with paint after investigating the roller pan. At the end of the after noon, the cleaning included the brushes, paint pan and dachshund noses. Carson arrived and announced that dinner would be at Tilly's that night. No cooking.

"It's on me," declared Carson.

Sheila said, "Oh, no, don't tell me this is another trade of yours, is it?"

"Nope," answered Carson. "Just got my social security check, we'll use real money. Respectable and all that. What a concept, huh?"

"Fair enough, then. But let's take the Camry. What does Tilly's have for dinner?"

Carson explained the soon to be divulged menu at Tilly's. "Well, you see, you're in Wisconsin here. They have what they call fish fry on Friday and today is Friday. Most places do a fish fry, some are better than others, but Tilly's is pretty nice. They've got slaw and potato pancakes and all that. Little lemon wedgies on the side. Good stuff.

Cirtron had a question. "Potato pancakes? How t'get de potatoes flat, mon?"

Redstripe and Paris had trotted in to where the humans were discussing dinner and knew they were hearing about food. *Ah, this sounds good. Fish, yeah. Slaw? Is that a vegetable? Not sure about that.*

Sheila had her own question. "What's this about a fish thing on a Friday? Is that some sort of local tradition, like clam digs or lobster boils or something? Where do they get fish around here big enough to eat anyway? Sounds a little odd."

Carson tried to answer both questions. "The potato pancakes, they grind 'em up and then fry them in little patty shapes. The fish comes in from other places, cod and haddock and all that, maybe a little perch from around here. But the Friday thing, that's a leftover from the Catholics. You'd have to live here a long while to understand it so, yes, I suppose it is a sort of local tradition. But the food, it's good. You'll like it. Get the ladies and we can take your car and go into town."

The trip to Tilly's was smooth. The air conditioning system in the Camry kept the humans and the dogs comfortable and no trucks or other vehicles on the road could throw stones in and upon the occupants. Sheila parked the car along the broken sidewalk in front of Tilly's and they all sauntered inside. Once the three were seated on the bar stools, the dachshunds let loose on the floor,

Carson called to Sue who was on duty for the dinner rush. "Three fish frys and three mugs, Sue. And something for the little ladies if you have anything. You'd better, or I'll let them loose on the bar top and they'll be sure to eat your patrol cat."

Sue reached for three mugs and began to fill them with beer from a tap. "Hey listen, Joe the cat can take care of himself. You watch he doesn't scratch those little dog's noses right off their little faces. Have I told you lately that you're impossible, Carson?"

Cats? Scratch US? No way. Let us at 'em! We'll get any cat around. Just tell us where it is. Cats are just disgusting. Yuck!

"Nope. You haven't. Have I told you lately that your burgers are better than a good laxative?"

Sue frowned a moment and then her face relaxed as she realized Carson was trying to get to her. She handed three beer filled mugs to Sheila, Cirtron and Carson in turn and replied. "No, Carson, you didn't tell me that. But that's a good thing to know as you are so full of it anyway. Nice to know we've been of some help."

Sheila tensed, waiting for some sort of outburst. Cirtron looked off in another direction. Sue and Carson were silent for just a second and then each laughed. "Sue?" said Carson, "You're all right, dear."

"So are you Carson. You're okay," Sue answered back.

Carson was not done. "Well, yes, I know that. I'm actually quite fine, thanks."

Sue laughed again, "Oh, enough! Shut up, you. I'll go and order up your fish. How about some bison jerky for the hounds? I'll get that myself."

From the floor, Redstripe was listening. *Jerky? That sounds a little dangerous.* Paris heard the offer as well but was thinking, *Bison? Yup, I could get into that.*

Cirtron, Sheila and Carson sipped their beers while the dachshunds craned their necks up to watch Joe the cat pad round and round the bar top. It was only a few minutes before the fish dinners arrived and Sue came out with two plates of bison jerky for the hounds. She placed them on the floor and the dogs each grabbed a strip in paws and jaws and began to chew. Above them, the humans dug into their own dinners. Carson watched Cirtron pick up a lemon wedge and bite into the entire fruit, gnawing it and peeling the rind off and away from his teeth.

"Cirtron!" admonished Carson. "You're supposed to squeeze that on the fish."

Sheila just held her hand to her eyes.

Cirtron said, "Ah, *ya*, mon. Not so as sweet as does back home."

As the dachshunds chewed and the three humans worked on their own plates, Sheila looked up and across the bar to notice the two men, again, with the baseball caps that had teased Cirtron during the last visit to Tilly's. They were snickering and pointing once more over the pizzas they had in front of them. They were not loud about it and had not yet made a nuisance of themselves, but Sheila worried about what might come. She decided to stem things quickly and said so to Cirtron and Carson.

Cirtron, the permanent pacifist, urged her to stay still. Carson told her to go ahead and knock herself out. Sue saw what was about to happen and leaned back, arms crossed, ready to be entertained. Sheila, once more, made her way around the bar and approached the two men.

"Hey. Remember me? I thought I'd come over and tell you I was sorry to give you a hard time about that belt buckle. I'm sure you understand I was just sticking up for my friend."

The first man looked up and said,"Uh yeah, that's okay. We didn't mean anything anyway. No harm, no foul, you know?"

The second man was quiet. He was worried about what might be coming.

"Well, anyway," said Sheila,"maybe you could give me your phone number? Would that be all right?"

"Oh! Yes! I can do that! Sue? Give me something to write with, would you?" Sue was quick to supply a pen and a clean napkin and the first man carefully wrote some numbers down and handed the paper to Sheila."There you are. I hope to hear from you!"

"Oh, I'm sorry. Maybe I didn't explain. You probably won't. Not directly. I thought I'd give your wife a call. I'm new here and am always looking for friends. But I'll be glad to tell her you were so nice to give me the number. Thank you so much." Sheila turned away and returned to Cirtron and Carson.

The second man, Sue the bartender and most of the other patrons in the bar erupted in laughter at the expense of the first man. Those that had not heard the exchange looked over and wondered what all the excitement was about. Redstripe and Paris began to bark, temporarily ignoring the bison jerky, and Carson was smiling. Joe the cat paused in his rounds. Cirtron gazed down at his potato pancake and wondered again how it had become flat.

Carson, wiping laughing tears from her eyes, told Sheila,"Honey, that was pretty good. I'm impressed. But you might want to go stick some money in that music maker over there and maybe take some of the pressure off. A little music always helps." Carson pointed at the machine holding CD's at the end of the room.

"Good enough, good idea." Sheila pulled a pair of dollar bills from a pocket and walked over to the player. Most the titles listed on the display were country western or light rock but she found a selection by Loggins and Messina called "The House at Pooh Corner." She let the machine suck in her bill and punched in the numbers on a pad. The lilting music filled the bar but it quickly became obvious that the other patrons were not impressed by the selection. People frowned and murmured as Sheila returned to her seat.

Cirtron noticed all of this and put a hand on Sheila's arm. "I can make dis better, mon. Here." He reached into a deep pocket of his pants and pulled out a wooden flute. Sheila had never seen it before. It was beautiful. A simple long hollow cylinder of wood with eight holes on top and two underneath, it had no apparent mouth piece. Both ends were open but a notch near one end was there to split blown air apart to make sound. The wood was multi grained with dark streaks like mahogany and lighter ones like teak. It appeared polished.

Sheila was awed. Carson leaned over to look. Sheila whispered, "What is that? Where did you get it? What are you going to do?"

"Be it my flute, m'lady. Made it in d'mountains. It be of d'wood of the hart of a tree called lignum vitae. It means d'wood of life, mon. Very good. Heavy and strong. Carves well, like iron but can be cut wid d'knife. I will play it, ok?"

Sheila could not find words but Carson said, "Play away there, Cirtron. Let's hear it."

Cirtron held one end of the flute to his lips and began to play. He used his fingers deftly over the holes to match exactly along with the music playing on the CD. The crowd in the bar, even the two men with the baseball caps, fell silent and listened. Cirtron's notes followed the tune precisely and when the CD track ended, he repeated the melody, only his flute making any sound in the room. Sheila was certain she saw his music carving clear notes in the smoke near the ceiling of the bar.

Cirtron finished, Redstripe and Paris began to howl from their spots on the floor and the room burst into the sound of applause. Cirtron pressed his palm to his head and then dropped his hand down, still open, as a salute and recognition. Sheila was stupefied.

Carson looked at Cirtron and said, "My, that was awfully good. But the dogs? I don't think they're gonna get first chairs in the woodwinds at the symphony orchestra."

Us? Don't sell us short, there. We can howl with the best, you know.

Nobody in town ever teased Cirtron again.

Wedding at Webb's

THE REMAINS of a bison roast that had been carved into thin slices lay on an oval plate. The meat was surrounded by a few unclaimed boiled potatoes and lonely fried carrots. Cirtron, Sheila and Carson were drinking the anise-laced coffee after their dinners while Redstripe and Paris busied themselves tongue-polishing their own dinner bowls now empty of dog chow that had been soaked in roast bison juices. The dog bowls clinked as little tongues lapped around them there in the kitchen of the Armstead Farm.

Carson placed her coffee mug on the table and wrapped both of her hands around it. She glanced over at Sheila and said "Say, girlie, 'mind cleaning up for us all tonight?" Carson did not wait for an answer before she continued, swiveling her head around to look at Cirtron. "Cirtron, ah, you know what? I should really show you how to work the frost plugs on the water supply lines for the drinking tanks in the pastures. If I don't do it now, I'll forget about it and come the first freeze, you'll have a problem. Come along, the plugs are in the shed."

Carson pushed her chair back, rose, and walked out the back door. Cirtron looked at Sheila, shrugged and followed the old woman out leaving an annoyed Sheila sitting among the soiled dishes while the two dachshunds looked up from the floor anticipating exercising their rights to help clean the supper plates.

In the back yard, Carson stopped and said to Cirtron, "Listen, forget the shed for now. I made that up. 'Just wanted to talk with you for a bit. And I think we'll need this." She pulled a small pipe, stuffed with trade, from a pocket and lit it with a butane lighter plucked out from the same spot. Placing it to her lips, she dragged on it briefly and while exhaling slowly handed it over to Cirtron. "Ah, then. That's better."

Cirtron took the pipe, inhaled and then, as he breathed back out said, "De talk, mon? Whad to be t'talk 'bout?"

"Cirtron, I'm not a person that usually interferes. Let it all be, that's me."

Cirtron doubted this but did not reply. He just sucked on the pipe again and handed it back.

"Ok," Carson went on, "here's the deal. If you haven't noticed it, your lady Sheila loves you." She held up a hand as if to stop traffic when Cirtron's eyes widened. "What you really need to do here is marry her and turn this double set of people and pups into a real family. It's a simple idea, really, Cirtron. But I wasn't so sure you were going to click on it yourself. So I'm here telling you. Understand?"

"Ah, mon. Not s'sure dis be de good thought. Dinna know 'bout it. Maybe I think 'pon dis."

"Well you *should* know about it and by all means, yes, you should, as you say, think upon it. Cirtron, if the whole idea got any closer to you, it'd bite you on the nose. And I'll tell you what; if you don't bring it up to Sheila, I will. So there you have it. Here," she handed the pipe back to Cirtron, "have a little more of that and just think it through." Carson turned and walked back to the house leaving Cirtron with the pipe and his thoughts.

Back in the kitchen, Sheila was finishing with washing, rinsing and drying the dishes. The hounds, sated finally, had headed for comfortable furniture in the front room. As Carson came back in, Sheila asked, "Did you get those pipe things taken care of with Cirtron?"

"I think so. He'll be back in a bit. I suppose we'll see if he really understood a little later on. I explained things as best I could. Tell you what, pour us some more coffee and let's go into the front room and I'll explain it all to you too."

THERE HAD BEEN a little bit of discussion about the clothing Cirtron and Sheila should wear at their wedding at Little Hills Lake. In the end, things were simple. Carson took Sheila up into the attic in the Carson farm house and pointed the tall blond to an old chest full of clothes. The two of them chose a long white muslin gown with wide, cuffed sleeves that smelled a bit of dust and mothballs. When Sheila tried it on she remarked that she felt a little bit like Shakespeare's Juliet. Carson commented that Cirtron did not look much like Romeo, but he would do and that Sheila looked just fine. The chest may have dated back to the Civil War and likely would have brought a better price at an antique shop than the entire contents.

Cirtron would choose sandals, a flowered shirt from home and a pair of long and stiff cotton pants he had found at the local hardware store. They were really painter's pants with big pouches and straps for tools, but they were clean and bright. Carson would weave wild flowers into wreaths for them both and that would complete the outfits. The trader planned on a sacky looking knee length cream colored smock and would wear her usual Nike running shoes. Her dress likely had started its life colored snow white but had aged to the darker shade over time. But it was one of the best things she had.

The dogs presented a more complex problem. Dachshunds do not dress up in their finest church- and go-to-meeting clothes with any cooperation. But a simple set of daisies, woven by Carson into collars for the hounds and barely to be noticed by the little prospective witnesses, would do just fine, thank you very much.

Previous to all of this wardrobe planning, one evening found all three of the humans at the kitchen table in the house on the Armstead Farm. It was just after dinner and the dachshunds were busy licking the remains of people dinner off of the plates that had been put down for them. Sheila was asking questions.

"Okay, if we are going to go through with this, there's some things we need to get straight. Where are we going to do this? Can we use some church around here? I suppose we'll need a minister and then there has to be some legal paperwork and all of that."

Carson had answers. "Camp Webb, Father Champaign, and I'll have one of my lawyer friends take care of the license and all that. Piece of cake."

Sheila was not convinced. "Camp Webb? Who is this Father Champaign guy? What about a marriage license, don't we need that?" The dachshunds continued to lick down below.

Carson sighed and Cirtron remained quiet. "Listen," said Carson, "Here's how it'll work. Camp Webb is a church camp on Little Hills Lake. The place is run by the Episcopal Church and it's over on that lake. Kids come up for the summer and they live in little cabins and get to swim, ride horses, make stuff and sail and canoe. They have a great time and come from all over, even as far away as Chicago. Father Champaign runs the place. They call him Father Champ. He'll be glad to do the ceremony, he owes me a favor anyway, and I know all the camp kids would be thrilled to be around for the festivities." The hounds had pretty much licked the dinner plates clean and Redstripe was pawing at Cirtron's leg and Paris was nosing against Sheila's. Out of habit, the two dogs were lifted up unto two laps.

Cirtron, holding Redstripe asked, "Dis man, de Father Champ? He owes d'favor mon?"

Sheila, holding Paris, opened her mouth to ask another question but Carson beat her to it. "Oh sure, Father Champ has been trading with me for years."

"Ya, mon, irie," replied Cirtron.

"Carson, I just give up," said Sheila.

Carson simply smiled and said, "Cirtron, how about you plan something to play on that flute of yours. I think that would be nice."

The next few days were filled as usual with the engine noises from the bobcat as Cirtron drove it around, more than really needed, and used it to lift the remaining hale bales up and over the fence for the bison. It really was not necessary as the big hay rounds had been delivered and the bison were chewing on those big wheels. But Cirtron did enjoy the bobcat. Carson had obtained the needed paperwork for the wedding, only the witness signatures were missing and of course Cirtron and Sheila would have to sign as well just after the ceremony planned at Camp Webb. At the end of the next week, on a late afternoon, Sheila, Cirtron and Carson dressed in their wedding day clothes and climbed into the Camry with the dachshunds for the short trip down the road to the camp.

At the camp they were met by Father Champ. He wore his black priest's shirt with the little bit of white showing out from his collar, black shorts and sandals. His hair was cropped short and close to his skull and a wide smile balanced a set of aviator sunglasses that covered his eyes above. He was tall. Very. "Hi! How are you Carson? This must be Sheila and Cirtron? Peace be with you all." He shook hands all around. The campers had gathered already, kids of the ages of eight to eighteen and looked on at the arriving wedding party. They pointed and whispered among themselves and a few of the older girls took a long look at Cirtron. A few older boys were staring at Sheila. Two of the younger girls approached and one handed Sheila a bouquet of wild flowers, the stems bound together with rough string, and the other reached up and placed a daisy in Cirtron's shirt pocket.

Once the hounds were lifted from the car and down onto the pine needle covered ground, Father Champ directed everyone over to the nearby amphitheater. It was simply a cleared circular area, the edges defined by rocks, and furnished with wooden benches. The campers seated themselves on the benches and Father Champ brought Cirtron, Sheila and Carson to the front. Redstripe and Paris, necks circled with their daisy chains, trotted along beside. *Lot's of people to play with here; maybe some have food.* Dachshund noses tested the air.

Hands placed on their shoulders, Father Champ gently turned Sheila and Cirtron to face the little crowd of campers. Carson turned as well and Champ stood towering at least a head over Cirtron and Sheila, two heads over Carson, and addressed the crowd. "God's afternoon, everyone!"

"God's afternoon," the campers recited back in unison.

"Ya, mon," said Cirtron.

"Hi there," said Sheila.

The priest called out to two of the older kids in the crowd. "Marylynn, Mike. You two come up, you can be witnesses and hold the two dogs, okay?" The teenagers rose, went forward and bent down to grab the hounds. *Ah, what's this? We were busy smelling things.* With Cirtron and Sheila in the middle, the two campers each on one side, dogs in arms and Carson standing as the matron of honor, Father Champ said quietly to Cirtron and Sheila, "You ready?"

"Ya, mon."

"Hi there," Sheila flushed a little, "I mean..yes."

Father Champ began. "We have been honored today to be able bear witness under God's eyes the joining of two into one. As we have all come to be here from different places, holding different ideas and dreams, so have these two people done. They seek to go forward, not as two different people, but as a pair bonded by trust and aspiring to live in concert under God. And also under *Ga*, as I understand it. Ask that they be blessed."

"Be blessed!" repeated the group.

Father Champ turned to Cirtron, "I believe we have some music?" Cirtron nodded, pulled his flute from his pocket, held it up to his lips and began to play. The notes began to be heard, they were slow to leave the flute and began to fly upward through the trees, butterflies in motion and rising toward light. It was a moment before Sheila recognized the melody but she did. It was an old song from the sixties. Where Cirtron had found it she had no idea, but Cirtron's wooden instrument was breathing out the song, "A Whiter Shade of Pale." The piece itself held little interest to the campers, they were too young to know of it even though they were fascinated with Cirtron's skill. But Sheila and Carson had to wipe at the corners of their eyes. Cirtron ended his performance with a long, low last note. The entire group stood awestruck and silent.

"All right, then," said Father Champ. "Everyone sit down, not you," he grinned at the wedding party, "let's go on." He had no paper, book or copied verse, he just began to speak. "Marriage is called a sacrament. It is a present from God, one that lets us be bound together in pairs, man and woman, and travel forward in life in such a way as to share the best of each other with one another. Over time, we also have the responsibility to take that sharing, that strengthening, and pass it on to others. This is what Cirtron and Sheila, Sheila and Cirtron, are promising today under the eyes of God and Ga. Yet this joining, this partnership, should never diminish the single spirit of either. A man and woman, a woman and man, should be like trees growing in the sunlight. They must thrive, bear their fruit, shelter those below them on the ground, but never allow one shadow to cast upon the other. Both are equal. But in the case of a strong wind, one shelters the other depending upon from which direction the storms come. So, Sheila, Cirtron, do you understand and make these promises?"

"Ya, mon."

"Yes, I do."

"Excellent," said Champ. "Do you have rings?" Cirtron and Sheila looked at each other and Sheila said, "Uh, no. We never thought of it."

Carson chimed in, "Well, I did. Here, she reached into a pocket and then held out two gold rings on her palm. These were mine and Mr. Carson's. You two should have them."

"Carson? No, we can't do that," Sheila protested.

"Yes you can, what am I gonna do with the darn things, anyway?"

Without speaking, Sheila took the rings, placed one on her finger and one on Cirtron's. He looked down at his hand and said, "I tank you, Carson."

"Now you are married," pronounced Champ, "Most people kiss about now."

Sheila and Cirtron kissed, the crowd of campers clapped and the two hounds, still bound in the arms of Marylynn and Micheal were thinking, *What in the world was THAT all about?*

Sheila and Cirtron stepped back from each other as the clapping faded away. Sheila said, "Uh, now what? Are we done?"

Father Champ laughed and said, "We are just about finished, yes. But we have go to over to the camp office and have you sign some papers. Marylynn and Micheal, you come too; you're going to sign as witnesses. Bring the dogs." He turned to Carson. "As the orchestrator of this marriage, we need you to sign as well so come along now." Champ took Carson by the arm and led the way out of the amphitheater and toward the office. The rest followed behind.

Half way down the path to the camp office, a few steps ahead of Cirtron and Sheila and the two hound bearing campers, Champ leaned over and whispered into the older lady's ear. "Say, Carson? About the trade?"

Looking straight ahead, Carson whispered back, "Hold your peace, Champaign, it's in the car. You know I keep my promises so just be still about it. Didn't they teach you patience at the seminary?"

"Oh, yes. I'm sure." Father Champ straitened up and, turning his head back over his shoulder said to the rest of the group, he proclaimed, "Isn't it a great day for a wedding?"

Inside the office, Father Champ directed the dogs be deposited on the floor and then directed the humans to a desk. He indicated papers and lines for signatures and explained who would need to sign where. Everyone signed as shown by Champ and he ended the process with a signature of his own. He bound up all the papers in a cardboard envelope and handed it to Cirtron. The outside had been pre-printed in black marker with "CIRTRON/ARMSTEAD" and the day's date. The father congratulated Cirtron with a handshake and Sheila with a kiss. "Go in god's peace and in Ga's."

Marylynn and Micheal were watching Redstripe and Paris devour one another's daisy chain collars. *Not bad for vegetables,* thought the dogs.

Carson spoke up. "Ok, I see the dogs have had their salads already so it's time for dinner for the rest of us. I'm taking Cirtron and Sheila to the Silver Bull. Father Champ, I'd be pleased to have you join us. Marylynn, Michael, care to join the party?"

Marylynn answered, "No, thank you very much, Mrs. Carson. We'd better stay here and we can keep the dogs if you want. They're cute and we can get them some of their own dinner. It'll be fun. Do they like hot dogs?"

Carson said, "I'm quite certain they'll suffer through. Thanks a lot."

The party arrived (the bride had to drive again) at the Silver Bull, Carson's choice for the post wedding dinner. Standing in the parking lot, Cirtron regarded the namesake symbol of the place with an open mouth. Facing the road to attract business, the hindquarters aimed at the front doors of the dining establishment, was a large bull constructed from clear, glass-like fiberglass. From inside of the creation, red lights lit the eyes of the bull and the body of the twelve foot long structure showed off white interior light like a transparent full moon. The clever creation looked indeed like a glowing silver bull; horns included. Cirtron recovered from his surprise, closed his mouth politely and then said, "Ya, mon, De big cow, de male, no? If we have such on de island, would not need de candles, lights or lanterns after de sun she sets. Pretty. But, maybe day may have de bison here as well."

Carson chuckled and said, "Don't worry about it, Cirtron. It's just an advertising thing and actually, I don't think the Silver Bull would put bison on the menu. It would upset the tourists." She took Sheila and Cirtron each by an elbow and directed them toward the front doors of the restaurant. "You coming, Champaign?" she asked the father. "Or are we all going to stand in this parking lot and get hungrier?" Father Champ trotted along obediently behind Carson and the two newlyweds.

Once all four were seated at the table that Carson had reserved, their waiter for the evening approached, identified himself as Alan, and proceeded to shake out the linen napkins from the table setting onto everyone's lap. Father Champ accepted the ministrations as did Shiela and Carson, but Cirtron grabbed the napkin and said, "Not to need d'help, mon. I can do it m'self. Irie."

"Very well, sir," said Alan. And then he handed a of menu to each that were expensive looking and nearly eighteen inches tall. "May I bring you a cocktail? A drink? While you look at the menu?"

Carson was the one to answer. "Alan, you can bring us a bottle of champagne. And four glasses. Keep an eye on the bottle and bring another when that one is gone. We're celebrating a wedding here, so make it nice, can you do that?"

"Ah yes, and congratulations to . . . ?" He looked at Father Champ, Carson, Sheila and Cirtron and did not know which were the bride and groom.

"Those two," said Carson pointing, "They just were married today."

"Ah, yes. My best wishes. This is wonderful. I'll bring the wine and then maybe you will be ready to order. No hurry. Please be at your leisure."

As Alan walked off Sheila leaned over to Carson and said quietly, "Carson, this place is very impressive, just great. I mean the linens and the sliver and all; it looks like a high class place back in New York." Sheila turned around and about to eye the brocaded wallpaper, the little lights installed at the top of the walls and the dark and perfectly polished woodwork that decorated the dining room. "But this is just too much. You shouldn't have done this!"

Sheila was not completely surprised, probably not surprised at all, when Carson told her, "Don't worry about it, I made a trade."

Before Sheila could say anything, Alan arrived with the champagne and four glasses. He filled them for each and said he would be right back for orders. It was Cirtron who made the first toast. He held his glass up and motioned for his new wife and the minister and their friend to do the same. "Hold on de glasses, m'friends and loves. I do remember today what de father has said 'bout de trees and shadows and storms and winds, mon. So it be for Sheila and me and all t'others so as Ga decides."

After that toast and a refill, the bottle was pretty much gone by the time Alan got back to take orders. Sheila recklessly ordered lobster, Carson asked for steak, and Father Champ politely asked for broiled chicken. Cirtron could not decide and requested chicken, steak and lobster. He ate every bit.

A second bottle of champagne was drained, accompanied by other toasts, and the wedding party toddled out of the Silver Bull over and to the car in the lot. No bill had been brought to the table. Carson had seen to all of that ahead of time. Sheila drove the car back to Camp Webb, dropped off the good Father Champ, and Marylynn and Michael brought out the hot dog saturated hounds to the car. Little dachshund bellies could be seen to be just a bit larger than usual. By the time that Cirtron, Carson and Sheila got back to the Armstead farm and Carson's place, everyone was pretty tired. Carson made her way back to her place and Sheila, Cirtron and Redstripe and Paris, climbed up the stairs to find the bed. Cirtron, who was not accustomed to champagne of any sort, plopped dead center in the middle of the bed. Redstripe and Paris clambered up, with help, and took positions one on each side of Cirtron. When Sheila came into the room, Cirtron lifted his head and said, "Ah, so sorry, m'lady. Dinna mean t'take the middle of de bed, mon. De dogs . . .

It was dark. The hounds were nearly asleep. Even dachshunds can have too much camp food. Sheila said, "You just stay right where you are, Cirtron, don't move. I have plans for you."

Redstripe and Paris woke from their dozing and peered up. *Can we help with something?*

Interlude on the Porch

CIRTRON WAS SITTING on the front porch boards of the house at the Armstead farm. It was nearly dusk, that time of day when the air is stilled and the world waits for the coming darkness. Cirtron could still see the highway at the end of the farm's driveway as he sat. Redstripe was in his lap, a little hound with her head on one of his knees while his legs cradled the little dog comfortably. Redstripe sighed and Cirtron did the same. The sighs had different meanings. Redstripe's was contented. Cirtron's was sad. Sheila came out from the house and onto the porch to see what was up. Paris followed out and began to nose at Redstripe for a spot on Cirtron's lap.

"What are you doing out here?" Sheila asked. Paris found a spot in which to curl along side Redstripe. Cirtron did not answer.

"The three of you are going to get cold out here. Why don't you bring the dogs in with you and we can watch some television or something. Wisconsin is not much different than New York and I can tell you it will be cold out here soon at this time of the year. It's not Jamaica, you know."

"Ya, mon. Is not Jamaica, no."

C'mon Cirtron, come inside," Sheila urged.

"Ah, I dun know 'bout it, just want t'tink a bit here."

"You miss the island, don't you?" asked Sheila.

"Ya, mon. Be dat true. I tink 'pon dat a great deal while de days go on."

"I'll tell you what, Cirtron, I know Carson would watch after the bison and dogs for a bit. Flights to Jamaica at this time are probably tough to find. How does Hawaii sound for a few days? It would be warm . . ."

The two dachshunds raised their heads. *Don't you think we are gonna stay here while you two go gallivanting around, you know. We know quite very well how to travel as you should remember. Don't even think about leaving us here with those big hairy things out back!*

Cirtron had his own answer. "No, mon, Hawaii. Is not so good as you see. Takes a lot of de money and de people not so happy as de television says. No."

"Cirtron, are you homesick?"

"Homesick? No mon, no home can give you de sickness. Just miss de island and all dat. De people here, day be different, nice people, but not as so. And de Sun, she not be so warm."

Sheila did not quite know what to say. She simply patted Cirtron on the shoulder, leaned down to kiss his head and said, "Look, I'll get you a blanket for out here and you just stay and think as long as you want. Should I take the dogs in?"

"Ya, mon. De blanket. But de little dogs can stay wid me, mon. Day jus wanna sleep.

"Good enough, Cirtron, I'll get a blanket. Maybe we can talk about all this later, alright?"

"Irie."

Doctor Aspin and Solutions

It was only two weeks after Cirtron and Sheila were married, had created a reasonably official family of two hounds and two humans, when there was a rapid knock on the front door of the house on the Armstead farm in the morning, way before coffee had even been brewed. Redstripe and Paris leaped from their covers on the bed upstairs and rushed down to sound the bark alarm and guard the door. Sheila heard the noises and rose to amble down in her rumpled nightclothes; eyes coated with the excretions of sleep, and opened the door.

"Can I help you? It's awfully early, what is it?"

Redstripe and Paris barked at and threatened a man standing outside the door. He had fresh jeans on and a work shirt. His feet were clad in rubber boots. He appeared to be a young person, slender, but his head of thick hair was nearly white; his complexion very pale. "Hi there!" he said. "I'm Doctor Aspin. I'm here to check on your bison. I can just go around the back but I wanted to let you know I was here."

Sheila, trying to muddle through the leftover numbness of a deep sleep, looked out in the front yard to see a pick up truck parked in the drive. "ASPIN VETERINARY" was painted on the driver's door. "Oh. Well. Yes. Please go ahead. We'll be out in a second after we get dressed." Redstripe and Paris, nudging at the door, continued to bark and scuff. "Would you two cool it!?" Sheila shouted down, "Settle, would you?"

The vet returned, "Hey, are those dachshunds? I wouldn't worry about them; they're fine, doing what they're supposed to. Did you know they were specifically bred for loud barks so that they could be heard when they dig through tunnels?"

"No, I didn't know that, but I'll tell you, with these two, I wouldn't mind putting them down in a tunnel now and then."

The doctor laughed and said, "Good enough, I'll see you out back." Redstripe and Paris gave loose a couple of indignant snorts. *Tunnels? We are not interested in tunnels. What we are interested in is breakfast!*

Sheila climbed back up the stairway, rousted Cirtron out of the bed and told him a vet was there to check on the bison, "We should go out and see what's up." Once dressed and out the back door, the two of them saw the vet inside the fencing and toeing around with the bison droppings. He scooped some samples into little plastic jars. The ever-present Carson was on her way over down the double rutted path in her golf cart. She stopped at the edge of the fencing and called out, "Hey Mike!"

The vet looked over and waved back. "I'm just here to check on things, just met the new owners!" He quit playing with the droppings and strode over to the edge of the pasture, the bison ignoring him, and climbed over and out. Redstripe and Paris approached slowly and snuffled at his rubber boots. "Things look all fine," he said to the assembled crew while looking down at the hounds.

Sheila and Cirtron, Carson at the side, stood in front of the doctor. Sheila asked, "How can you tell?"

The vet explained as he reached down to pat at the hounds. "In the case of bison, it's rather simple. You really can't do much with them anyway. Generally they don't need the injections and other treatments like dairy cows or beef cattle or horses. And it is pretty difficult to treat them. They are so primitive. Even getting them into a trailer is tough, their skulls are so thick and strong, they can dent the inside of a horse trailer like a tornado inside a can of tuna. What I do, unless I see lesions or cuts on them somewhere that warrants an antibiotic, is to check their dung. If it's pretty dry and there aren't any creepy crawlies in it, things are probably okay. It looks like your herd is fine today." He shook off some bison dung that had clung to a boot and the dachshunds pursued it to where it landed in the grass. They gave a new definition for the term "brown nosing."

Cirtron asked, "You take de care of de animals all 'round den?"

Aspin answered, "Yes, the big ones are my specialty. I take care of my clients' horses and cows and, of course, your bison. I like the big ones. It used to be that I shared a practice in a little town called Hartland with my brother. He's a vet too. But I came up here to work with the larger animals and left my brother to deal with all the cats and dogs that the rich people down there would bring in. It has worked out for both of us."

Cirtron nodded. "Ya, mon. You do de big ones, and your brother, he do de small, like de dachshunds?"

"Yes," replied Aspin. "That's pretty much it, although I treat the occasional cat or dog if someone needs me too and can't find another vet. Once, as an example, there was this guy who came in. His cat had gotten into his tackle box and got a fishing lure stuck in the skin around its mouth. The guy put the poor cat in his lap and drove over to see me, but by the time he got to my office, the cat had wriggled around, got the lure that stuck in its face stuck to its paw and then stuck again right into the poor fellow's groin. You had to see it. This man comes in with a cat stuck in his lap. The cat's howling and the guy can't stand up straight. I few snips with pliers took care of it all but that was something."

While Sheila laughed, the dachshunds looked up. *Cats? What's this again about cats?* Cirtron had walked away and took up a position down the fence line and just gazed out at the herd, his arms folded against his chest.

Carson said, "Mike, you keep telling that cat lure story. Aren't you going to get any new ones?" The dachshunds had approached Aspin again at ankle level and used noses to show their fascination with the clods still stuck the to veterinarians boots. Before the man could protest, Carson said to Sheila, "Hey, what's with Cirtron this morning? He off his feed or something?"

Sheila glanced over at her Jamaican husband and said, "No, well maybe. I think he's homesick."

"Homesick?" asked Mike Aspin, "Where is he from?"

"Jamaica, he's a rastamafarian," offered Sheila.

"I know that place; it's in Illinois, right? I've been there I think. Rastamafarian? I remember a pizza place with that name there," said the vet.

"Mike," Carson told him, "you are an unmitigated fool. Jamaica is in the Caribbean south of Cuba and a rastamafarian is someone who holds to certain beliefs. It has nothing to do with pizza. I think you really ought to stick with groping cows, I really do. You'll never make it as a travel agent. Sheila, let's go inside and talk about this homesick thing over some coffee. Mike? If you promise not to tell more stupid stories, you can come along too." Carson headed for the house, Mike and Sheila following behind, and the dachshunds trotted over to keep the brooding Cirtron company. They were thinking that *Cirtron could use a good lick on the nose, or maybe some dog cookies. Or maybe he should just go and bite a cat, yeah, that would be good. There is nothing like biting a cat to improve your point of view!*

Over coffee and while Mike Aspin was preparing a bill for his service to the bison, Carson listened to Sheila explain that Cirtron had told her he was not as happy as could be living on the bison farm and in the little town of Wautoma. Sheila tapped her fingers on the side of her coffee cup while Carson rendered an opinion."You have to go to Jamaica, girlie. That's just it. Stay here and Cirtron is just going to get buried in resentment. Besides, you like Jamaica, don't you?"

Sheila had doubts. "I do, I really do. I'd love to go back there, but the farm and the dachshunds and all that; I can't see a way to get that all taken care of and just leave. Dr. Aspin? I know it is a problem to take dogs to a foreign country, but do you know of a way to make that happen? I can't possibly leave them here. They're family. And what about the bison?"

The vet answered, pushing the bison dropping samples he'd brought in to one side."What you need to do is get the right forms filled out and filed, I can do that, and the little hounds would be probably placed in quarantine for a while. It's a tough thing. I don't know about Jamaica, but it could be as much as four weeks or more. There are some exceptions for show animals and all of that, but I am pretty sure that is what you would be looking at if you want to take the dogs. As far as the bison are concerned, there are a couple of other ranches in the state that would be more than happy to buy them from you. That part is easy."

"Mike?" asked Carson,"isn't there another way for the dogs?"

"No," said the vet,"unless you are some high and mighty movie star or some big politician, the rules always apply about transporting dogs from one country to another."

Carson perked up. "Politicians. Yes, that might be it. Let me make a few calls. Sheila, Mike has given me an idea. Let me see what I can do. And I'll call Pederson at the bank. I tell him to take care of selling your place and Mike here can contact some folks about buying the herd. Right Mike?"

"Sure, I can do that. Give me a few days, okay?"

Cirtron and the dogs wandered into the kitchen through the back door. "Waz up?" he asked.

Sheila smiled at him and said, "You said you didn't like Hawaii. What do you say to Negril? Carson says she can fix it with a little help from Dr. Aspin here. What do you say we go home?"

Cirtron froze for a moment and then his face broke into a bright smile. "De dogs, mon. Not to leave widout de dachshunds, mon. De bison, though, too big t'take along."

Carson rose from the kitchen table and said to Cirtron, "Well, of course not you hairy thing. Do you think I want to stay here and watch these two little carpet crawlers forever? They are way too much trouble for an old lady." Redstripe and Paris started to bark. "See what I mean?"

In the next few days, Carson had worked her magic, mostly based on trade agreements, and had procured promises from high level government officials to forward papers for the dogs. Redstripe and Paris would be allowed to travel to the Caribbean and enter Jamaica with the quarantine requirements waved. She'd also talked to her favorite banker.

"Tom?" she'd spoken to him over the phone. "I have something to tell you. Your bank is going to buy the Armstead place and issue a check to Sheila Armstead. Pick you price, just make sure it is at least the last appraisal number; you should still have that in your files."

The banker said stiffly, "Rose, you must know I can't do that. I have people to which I must answer. This is just too irregular. I'm sorry, but, no, I simply cannot approve such a thing."

Carson was firm, "Tom, you are going to do just that or I will stop trading with you. It is up to you, it's your choice, so what do you say?"

Pederson was silent for just a moment but said, resigned, "All right. You have a hard attitude, Rose, but I will take care of this. I only hope no one asks me any specific questions. And I want you to remember something. This time you owe me, I don't owe you. Is that satisfactory?"

"Perfect as a peanut, Tom. Thank you."

Later, in the shadow of a waning afternoon, Carson invited Cirtron and Sheila and the hounds over to her place next door. She explained how things would work and that the traveling papers for Redstripe and Paris should arrive shortly. All that needed to happen was to get the check from Pederson. Sheila had one more question. "I can't believe what you've done. And all from trade? You are an amazing lady. I did check the airlines though, the only flight we can get to Jamaica, to Montego Bay, is out of Chicago. I'm not crazy about driving all of the way there, even with Cirtron to help, with the two back seat barkers. Once was enough."

Carson, the virtual encyclopedia of anwers said, "That's not a problem. Wautoma has a little airport and you can charter a single engine plane down to the windy city. It'll be a nice view. Those little planes fly pretty close to the ground, not like the jets."

Goodbye

SHEILA AND CIRTRON and the dogs, Carson in the back seat of the Camry, drove out to the little airport on a fresh October morning. Carson held the dogs on the short trip. The airport was just a wide strip of grass used for landings and takeoffs with a long hanger off to the side. A single wind sock hung on a pole for pilots to judge the local conditions. A dozen little planes were parked on the side, big and brightly colored moths resting in the grass. A quick trip to a small office, equipped with fans, was all that was needed to complete arrangements and payment for the flight to Chicago.

Once outside the little office, the group looked out to the grass runway where a female pilot, her ears covered with headphones, was waving at them as she stood next to a small plane. Sheila thought she looked, with the headgear, a little like a high tech Minnie Mouse.

Sheila was the first to speak. "Well, I guess it's time to go. Rose Carson, I don't know a good way to thank you for all you've done for us. You drive me nuts, you know, but what you've done is . . ."

This time, Carson had the chance to interrupt Sheila, "Honey, it has been a pleasure. It's been loads better than just sitting on my duff out at my place all by my self. Don't give it a thought. You two just take care of yourselves, and take care of the dachshunds." She placed a hand on each of Sheila's arms and stood tiptoe to be able to kiss her on the chin. Carson's eyes were welling up just a bit as were Sheila's. Carson stood back and turned to Cirtron, "And you, my good man, I must say I have never had the joy of meeting anyone like you. Go with God and be happy, Cirtron. Take good care of the girlie here. And don't forget to play your flute now and then, ok?" Carson raised her eye glasses and wiped at her tears with the back of one hand.

"No need for de tears, mon. De parting of de friends is to be a time to be happy to tink on de meeting later on. You see dat it is not sad."

"Those are not tears, Cirtron," Carson argued, "my allergies are acting up. Happens all the time." She sniffed and cleared her throat.

"Ah, so may it be dat. But y'know little lady? From what I learned, de allergies, day not come so dis part of de year, mon."

"Oh, shut up, Cirtron." Carson was embarrassed, a rare thing to have happen.

"Ya, mon. And so." Cirtron smiled a broad smile looking down on Carson. "I have de thought. Y'come and be wid us soon. We find de place on de island, get some ah de chickens and de goats mon, make a place t'live happy, mon. You come soon. Not cold dere. Always hot. Even de rain, she be hot."

This time Carson let the tears flow down her cheeks and reached to hug Cirtron; her head just below his chin. "Thanks, buddy, that is such a dear thought. But I'm too old to . . ."

It was Cirtron's turn to interrupt. "Not to listen 'bout de old ting. No matter. Long as we breath and love under the gaze of Ga, den, young? Old? N'matter. T'tink another way is not t'have de common sense, mon. You tink on dis as I say and you come soon, mon."

Startled by her own feelings, Carson said, "Ok, I'll think about it. You guys will have to tell me where you light anyway. I'll have papers and such from the sale of the farm to send you." She reached down, groaning and gasping just a bit, to lift each one of the dachshunds up. She held first Paris, then Redstripe and kissed each one on the end of their long little noses. "You girls be good. I'll miss you little trouble makers!"

Back on the ground, both of the dachshunds snorted and tried to shake off the moisture from Carson's kisses from their snouts. "You know what you two little furry fiends?" said Carson, "you two just have no respect."

With little left to say, promises hovering in the air and feelings rising up into the cool morning sky, Cirtron and Sheila grabbed the hounds and headed out to the little plane. Carson called out suddenly shouting, "Wait! Wait! What about the car?"

Sheila staggered mentally for just a second. She'd forgotten about the Camry. It certainly was not going to packed in luggage or shipped over seas. She made a quick decision and shouted back, "Keep it Carson, the title's in the glove compartment. Park that damn golf cart of yours and drive like a real person!"

O'Hare International Airport: 3 AM

The Dachshunds Save Chicago

RAINDROPS HIT, clung and then raced downward to the sill on the outside of a window of a hotel room near O'Hare in Chicago. Nearby, within sight of the Helios Winds building, the airport was mostly quiet at three in the morning. The runways and boarding gates and check-in counters would not begin to visibly bustle until just before the sun began to rise. Inside room 356, behind a carefully locked door, two men huddled over a small suitcase that was open on a bed.

"Hey, pay attention," said one of the men to a third who was seated at a table spread with food, "Hand me that battery."

Reaching into his shirt pocket, the third man stood and took a few steps away from the small round table that occupied a place near the rain spattered window. He handed over a small nine volt battery.

A soft click was heard as the battery was clipped in place.

"Try it."

The third man took a small, cell-phone sized device from his pants pocket and touched a button. A corresponding light lit on the surface of a small box in the suitcase.

"Ah, we are in luck, it works. But the battery may be loose. It might rattle."

The third man had returned to the table and had seated himself so as to continue to decimate the pile of fast food. He plucked a greasy paper from a pile of discarded wrappers.

"Here," he offered, "take this, wind it around the battery and stuff it in." He rose again and strode to the bed, handing over the paper that that had been wrapped around a barbecue sandwich.

The battery was secured. The little battery and box with the light were buried deep under clothing. A jar of peanut butter was placed on top. While the box and battery might alert the baggage scanning equipment at the airport, a hand search would expose the peanut butter first and the threat would be assumed false. Peanut butter was known to set off the alerts on the scanning equipment in airports as it had a similar consistency to the x-ray signature for certain kinds of plastic explosives. The suitcase was closed and left unlocked so as to avoid suspicion. The three men began their wait.

Across the hallway, in room 357, the two small dogs and Cirtron and Sheila slept. The front desk had a wakeup call placed on record in the hotel's automated system for those occupants of room 357 for four o'clock in the morning. A medium sized dog crate rested just inside the hotel room door and two small carry-on suitcases, one with an envelope of tickets and diplomatic papers for Inter-Caribbean flight 4330 to Jamaica inside, kept the crate company.

In room 356 the three men needed no wake up call.

O'Hare waited in the dark for the next morning of flights and the daily commotion of travelers. Cirtron, Sheila, Redstripe and Paris continued to snooze. The dogs dreamed of rabbits and gophers and cats. They twitched and whined in their sleep, imagining chasing little animals in their dog-designed dreams. Sheila had nightmarish visions of bison roaming the hills of Jamaica and snoring Cirtron just slept; his mind blissfully at rest and in its usual state. At four o'clock in the morning the wake up call, a shrill sound from the motel room phone, gave all four of them a start; a painful awakening in the morning darkness. Mr. and Mrs. Cirtron groaned and climbed out of bed. The dachshunds had to be mined out from under the blankets. Once the dogs were fed, Sheila and Cirtron showered and the toiletries packed, the four of them, on a total of twelve paws and feet between them all, trundled out of the room, down an elevator, and into the lobby.

The three men from room 356 were already there and waiting for the airport shuttle that would take them all over to O'Hare. Each man had a small carry on. One of them held the suitcase with the small device and battery. The other two also had similar small suitcases packed only with clothes and travel items that would serve to help make them appear as normal travelers. All three had passports and tickets tucked into pockets in their clothes.

Outside the lobby, the October early morning air was chilly. Redstripe and Paris balked at leaving the warmth of the lobby and there was a moment when the dogs stopped, planted their paws and refused to go forward through the door. While Cirtron carried the luggage, Sheila, two strained leashes in hand, gave in and plucked each hound up and carried them out. She took them both out to a convenient strip of lawn and put them down. Neither dachshund was at all pleased having to stand in the dewy grass and let their thoughts be known by snorting and grunting. *This is just too much and way too early! Our paws are all wet! And our tummies aren't much better. What is all this, anyway?* Sheila just let them finish their dachshund business and walked them over to the shuttle van where Cirtron was waiting and the three men were already on board.

Once both dogs and Cirtron and Sheila were on the shuttle, the driver asked which airline all were connecting with so that he would know at which terminal gates to stop. The ride over the much-used road to the airport was a rattly, jostling thing and reminded Sheila of Carson's golf cart. The dachshunds were not having a good time.

Cirtron, Sheila, the dachshunds and the three men all left the van at the same terminal. They were ticketed for the same flight. Once inside the airport, eyes trying to adjust to the bright indoor lighting, they headed for the check in counter for Inter Caribbean Airlines. A line of waiting passengers had already formed. All the baggage would be checked, but the three men would not board. Everyone in line waited, shuffled forward, dragging suitcases, and the dogs followed along reluctantly.

A young man and young woman approached the Cirtrons and dogs. They wore blue shirts and dark pants. A label on the sleeve of each of their shirts read "SKY PETS."

The woman spoke first and addressed Sheila. "You must be Sheila Armstead? And these are the dogs? Oh aren't they just so cute? Don't you love them? We're here to arrange their transfer by air to Montego Bay? We'd like to thank you for using the services of Sky Pets?"

Bleary eyed and sleep deprived, Sheila wondered if the woman could talk without a question mark. She wanted to say to her, "*Yes, I'm Sheila, these are the dogs, yes they are cute. Your name wouldn't happen to be Buffy, would it?*" She restrained herself and said, "Yes, I'm Sheila, thanks for meeting us here. We've got the travel crate and the papers here for you."

The young man spoke. "Great. We need to see those papers but really we don't need the crate. We use our own custom designed transports. They are designed especially each for every breed of dog. They will be perfectly safe and secure in the heated and pressurized section of the luggage bay. Gloria here will be flying with you in the cabin should any need at all arise. We just need to see your papers for the dogs, have you sign some things, show us your identification and we'll take the dogs with us up ahead." The man produced a clipboard, Sheila withdrew a set of papers from a pocket on her carry on and handed them over to the woman who began to read them. Cirtron remained quiet and just looked on.

"Oh my, isn't this something? You have diplomatic permits for the dogs? Tim, how often do we see this?" She turned to Sheila. "So, the dogs won't be going into quarantine then?"

Redstripe and Paris were busy wrapping their leads around Sheila's ankles while she gritted her teeth and simply said, "No. Show me where to sign."

With the paperwork completed, Tim and Gloria from Sky Pets collected the two dachshunds, one with Paris and one with Redstripe and carried them off. The departure was sudden and Sheila stood a moment, feeling lost, watching the dogs look back over the shoulders of the two young people. The dachshunds did not look happy. Sheila said, without turning to Cirtron and staring at the receding dogs, "Do you think they'll be okay? I mean, well, they just took them!"

"Ya, mon. Not t'be de one wid de worries, mon. Be it better than traveling in de bag wid no air."

A few minutes later Cirtron and Sheila reached the counter, presented their tickets and passports and received their boarding passes, seat assignments and baggage claim tags. The three men were right behind them and checked in as the two bound for Jamaica left the counter and headed for the boarding gate. But the three men did not follow. Boarding passes in their hands, their baggage checked, they headed back out the front doors of the airport and boarded a little bus back to the Helios Winds hotel. No one noticed.

Worrying about the dachshunds now in the care of Gloria (Buffy) and Tim from Sky Pets, Sheila made her way to the departure gate for flight 4330. Cirtron walked alongside her, happy to be on his way back to Jamaica. Once at the gate, it was not long before the two boarded, took their seats and settled in for the flight. To Sheila's delight, Gloria was not in a seat near theirs. Redstripe and Paris were down below, not in good moods, but safe and sound and warm. The plane rolled away from the terminal, guided by the guys with the big flashlights, paused at the end of one of the many runways and took off. The vibrations of the take off had the dachshunds up and on their feet inside their little cage thinking, *This is NOT fun. We'd take Carson's golf cart any old day. This is just ridiculous, we're not even hungry. Humph!* The dogs pawed at their ears as the pressure in the hold changed with the plane's rise into the early morning sky.

The three men had returned to their hotel room and were watching out the window; the view included the runway used by flight 4330. They'd planned that.

As the plane rose, the dachshunds pawed their ears, the three men watched and Sheila and Cirtron were listening to the drone of a flight attendant explaining seat belts and safety regulations for the flight, a phone rang in an office at 219 South Dearborn Street in the City of Chicago, the Chicago Divisional Offices of the Federal Bureau of Investigation. Outside calls to that office were not supposed to go through. The caller must have had access to some very special information.

"Ruminiski," answered the occupant of the office.

The caller was brief. "There is a problem on flight 4330 out of Chicago and headed for Montego Bay. I know this. Check room 356 at the Helios." The line went silent.

In the special cargo hold of the flight for Montego Bay, Redstripe and Paris were worrying the clasp that held their little prison shut. The "specially designed transport" cage fell open after just a few moments of pawing and gnawing by persistent dachshunds. The two were quickly loose in the compartment and sniffing around their surroundings.

Ruminiski acted immediately. Taking the call as real because it had come straight to his desk, he gave its legitimacy no thought at all. Besides, he knew that voice. He punched a few buttons on the phone and spoke rapidly. "I need two special forces units to the Helios Hotel and two to the airport. Do it now, do it five minutes ago! I'll have info to radio them on their way." He left his office not waiting for an answer and headed to another room used for communication with the various resources of the FBI.

The three men in room 356 watched the airplane begin its ascent.

Redstripe and Paris, ambling around among cases and crates and packages, found one of the suitcases from the three men. It smelled pretty good. *Ah hah! There must be something good in here. Let's get it!* They began to use teeth and claws on the case. The suitcase latches failed as quickly as the cage latch and the two dogs began to nose around inside, searching for something to eat. There is nothing like the possibility of food to motivate a dachshund. Paws dug and piled clothing out in all directions.

Deep in the bowels of the O'Hare airport, the air traffic control room senior supervisor received a call he did not want. The voice on the other end of the line cited a code phrase, identifying himself as FBI and then his instructions were brusque and clipped. "Get the pilot on flight 4330 to return to his departure point. Hold off all incoming traffic. Hold all aircraft at their gates and stop those out waiting to take off. Shut it down. Shut it all down. Get that 4330 back on the ground. Get it down now! We're on our way."

Paris's nose found the wrapper soaked in grease. Redstripe's nose was right along side. Each hound clamped her teeth on the paper and pulled back, ripping the thing in two. Redstripe's half was still stuck to the battery and she shook it as if she had just clamped down onto some hapless gopher. The force of the shake tore the battery from its connection and the little light on the box went dark.

In the control room, the senior supervisor issued his directions and the air controllers fell to the task of trying to stop an entire airport. They could do it. They were well trained, but many armpits began to darken. No voices were raised, but heartbeats thrummed in the chests of everyone in the room. All along the concourses of the airport, the ceiling hung flight information monitors began to change. Where flights had messages reading "ON TIME" or "ARRV 8:00 AM" or "BOARDING," the displays, one by one changed to "DELAYED," "DELAYED," DELAYED." Groans and curses could be heard all along the concourses as the words changed.

Two large dark trucks arrived at the Helios. Men and women in armor and helmets and carrying automatic weapons swarmed out and into the hotel. Not even stopping to tell the management what was going on, several took up positions to block the elevators. Two separate groups rushed up the stairways. Several ran to the rear and stood to guard the back of the building. Two men in windbreakers with FBI in yellow letters on the back followed in and stayed in the lobby. It was a frightening display made more so because they were all so quiet. Several guests in the lobby dropped half full coffee cups and froze in place before they were rounded up and led outside.

On board flight 4330, the captain received the message from air traffic control. He was told to turn around, that the airways had been cleared and to descend at his own discretion. He was also told not to spare the passengers. His second in command heard this and began to make preparations while informing the flight attendants they would be returning to their departure point. The descent might be a little rough. He turned to the captain and said, "This is no way to start a day."

"I've had better ones," replied the captain. "Guess we won't need the flight plan book." Both men were shaking but refused to share their fear.

The second in command keyed the intercom to the passenger cabin. His voice was calm and friendly even while his adrenal glands were pumping out anxiety juice. "Good morning, ladies and gentlemen. I want to thank you today for flying with us on Inter Caribbean Flight 4330 with service from Chicago to Montego Bay." He clicked off the mike for a moment to help maintain his calm and then started again. "We've just received a request to return to the Chicago Airport, just a routine double check on our radio equipment. This has nothing to do with the airworthiness of our aircraft today and the delay will add just a few minutes to our trip." He did not feel guilty about lying through his teeth. He continued. "The captain asks that you make certain your seatbelts remain fastened, your trays in the upright position. Please ask the flight attendants if you need any help at all, they will be glad to assist you."

In room 356 at the Helios, the three men could still see the airplane in the distance. The first man just watched, the second one had binoculars and the third held the little cell phone like device. "Now," said the first man. The third pressed a button.

Nothing happened. The third man pressed the button again. And then again. "What's wrong!?" he wailed.

"Wait," said the first. "Just wait, it won't be right away." The second continued to gaze through the binoculars.

The dachshunds were happily chewing and lapping at the greasy wrapper. The captain banked the plane sharply and the passengers could feel the plane vibrate and hear it groan as they were pressed into their seats by the tight turn of the aircraft. Most gripped the arms of their seats tightly and many began to shout. Down below, Redstripe and Paris were thrown over and away from the opened suitcase, bumping and sliding around in the compartment and scrabbling for a solid purchase to stand.

"See?" said the first man at the hotel room window, "Look at the con-trail, its curving, the plane is beginning to turn. Watch now, it worked."

But the plane just continued to turn smoothly and began downward in an even but steep path, arrowing straight back for the runways. "Give me that sender!" shouted the first man. He grabbed the device and stabbed at the button frantically. "It can't be!" He tried slamming the thing down repeatedly on the table and punching the button again. He had no time left to experiment or wonder. The door shattered open with an explosive bang and the helmeted, armored and weapon carrying special forces team filled the room. One man shouldered through the group from the rear and snatched the sending device.

Behind the shield of his helmet, his face was one huge grin. "I hope you won't insult us by asking for a warrant." He held up the little device. "We've go it right here."

As the bad guys (as the FBI called them privately) were taken down, the airplane bearing the hounds and Sheila and Cirtron was coming down too. It dropped steeply from the sky and the heaviness the passengers had felt in the turn now changed to the feeling of being in a descending elevator that was in way too much of a hurry. Unsecured objects began to fly around the cabin and people were screaming. Sheila turned in a panic to Cirtron but there was too much noise to make herself heard. Her heart was in her throat and then seemed to drop back down to her shoes when she thought of the two dogs below. Redstripe and Paris went weightless for just a moment, probably the first dachshunds to really fly, and then plopped back down into a tumble of crates and suitcases as the pilot raised the nose of the plane to a position ready for the landing. They didn't even have a chance to bark. Wheels down at the last moment, the pilot brought the plane down onto the runway hard. The wheels screamed and smoked. But they were down and rolling toward the special forces trucks at the end of the runway. The plane stopped, engines still whining, and was immediately surrounded. The passenger cabin was perfect bedlam.

The Special Forces team had spread themselves around the plane quickly. Two members were up front aiming their weapons at the windows of the cockpit and were relieved when both pilots held up their fists with thumbs extended. That was a good sign. Several more pushed stairways to the two passenger doors and others brought ladders up to the baggage area access hatches. The first hatch was opened wide while more team members aimed weapons at it. Two little dachshund faces appeared and looked down, two little sparrows peering from a birdhouse.

The people on the ground paused, shocked. A couple of them lowered their weapons, others began to chuckle and one was heard to say, "What on God's earth?" Redstripe and Paris just looked. It was a long way to the ground. Two men were directed by a commander to climb up and inspect and secure the baggage compartment.

"Climb in there, but first hand those two dogs down. I don't know what they have to do with this, but get 'em down here." Two men climbed the ladder and the first grabbed Redstripe, then Paris, and handed the dogs in turn down the ladder. They were given over to a big guy who had to stand with the squirming dachshunds held tight against his body armor, one under each arm. He was not pleased. "Why me?" he grumbled.

Why us? thought the hounds.

Inside the plane, the two men looked around. They saw tumbled containers, an open suitcase and a dog crate with its door ajar. A few scraps of paper littered the floor. One man leaned down to look into the suitcase and saw the box with the now darkened lights. Two broken wires protruded from one side. The other man bent down and retrieved the battery where it had landed on the flooring. Two wires from the battery matched those on the box in the suitcase. Both stood and one looked from the suitcase, to the dog crate and then back. He placed his hands on his hips, threw his head back and began to laugh.

Still laughing, he turned to his partner and said, "Marty, I think I know what happened here! Boy, you know I hate these things, but this time, this is an absolute circus! Check around, but I think we're okay here. I've got to see if there are some names on that crate. We'll want to find the dogs' owners but this is unbelievable. The perpetrators here were doomed by dachshunds. I can't stand it!" He looked at Marty who seemed confused and said, "Don't worry about it, just check around. I'll tell 'em outside we're set, just to have the guys get this thing out of here and make sure it's safe." He went over to the crate and scribbled names on a pad from his pocket;

Cirtron/Armstead-Seats 16D 16E. Still laughing softly, he had to wipe his eyes before he climbed out and down to the surface of the runway. He began to explain what he thought to his commander as Agent Ruminiski strode up. Both the commander and Ruminiski listened; they'd heard lots of odd stories and neither one frowned or smiled.

Ruminiski addressed the field commander, "He may be right. I hope he's right. We have the bad guys and it looks like they only had one device. If this is it, we've got it sacked. The manifest has been checked, there are no other accomplices that we can uncover. Let's get these people off the plane, finish securing it, but first let's talk to these dog owners. Have someone go get them off the plane." The commander nodded to the agent that had found the suitcase and device. The man headed off to retrieve Cirtron and Sheila. Off to the side, the big guy holding Redstripe and Paris coughed for attention.

"Hold your horses, fella," said Ruminiski.

"I believe they are dogs, sir," said the hound's temporary handler.

Ruminiski just glared.

Redstripe and Paris just squirmed.

The flight attendants were called to the front of the plane and asked to please have the passengers in seats 16D and 16E come forward. Sheila and Cirtron were led out of the plane and down onto the runway where the big guy with the hounds and the commander and agent waited. The passenger cabin had gone quiet. The men explained what they believed had happened. Sheila and Cirtron listened while Sheila kept looking over at Redstripe and Paris in the arms of the armored gargantuan and then finally asked, "This phone call you received, how did this person know this was a problem? Who is he, can we thank him?"

The commander pointed to a man wearing a White Sox jacket and baseball cap who was leaning against one of the trucks, his hands in his pockets. Dark glasses and the brim of the cap made his face invisible. "That's him. But I don't know his name. I'm not supposed to. No one is."

The man touched a hand to the brim of his cap, waved, and then turned and walked away. Redstripe and Paris were handed back to Sheila and Cirtron.

Ruminiski looked at Paris and Sheila and the hounds. "I really should ask you to come back to the offices with me and ask some questions and check on some things. This is one of more bizarre things I've seen. And I do want to thank you. But I suppose as it seems things are all in hand here, you two can be on your way. The four of you, that is."

Breaking a long silence Cirtron asked, "Ah, ya, mon. But de plane? I would not have de tought she be gonna go someplace soon, mon. It was our trip t'home for me, mon."

Sheila wanted to tell Cirtron to just keep still and that they should just get out of there as soon as possible. But Ruminiski said, "Well, you're right. This plane is not going anywhere. Not today anyway. The airlines will have to find these passengers other flights and that is going to take a while. But I'll tell you what. It'll be the least we can do here. Let me have your passports and I'll take them over and have someone run the numbers through over one of the computers in our trucks. I assume they'll be clear and we'll find a way to get you to, where were you going, oh yeah, Montego Bay. It'll be on us. Fair enough?"

"The dogs too?" asked Sheila.

"The dogs too," answered Ruminiski. "But what do you say we have them ride up top this time?"

"Ya, mon," said Cirtron.

"Sounds good by me," said Sheila. "What do you ladies think?" she asked the dogs.

"*Woof.*"

ARRANGEMENTS WERE made and a car was brought for Sheila and the dogs and Cirtron to take them from the runway and back to the terminal. Besides the driver, two agents accompanied the group. Each wore a dark windbreaker with the FBI letters on the back, sunglasses, jeans and clean running shoes. They could have served as bookends. The car stopped near an "Authorized Personnel Only" door and everyone got out. As one agent held open the door, his partner said, "Take it easy now. We have to go up through one concourse and then down another to get to the gate we need. There is likely to be some media people around. Things like this have a way of leaking out quickly."

In the door and up a set of stairs, they all went through one more door and out unto the carpet of concourse six. The place was packed with people whose flights had been delayed because of the fate of flight 4330. "C'mon folks, let's go. We'll carry the dogs."

Each agent picked up a dachshund and held it in both arms, a nose sticking out on one side and a tail on the other. "Stay right behind us." Redstripe and Paris tried briefly to wriggle but quickly found they were clamped down tightly. They were safe, but were not too crazy about the travel arrangements.

Word had indeed leaked out. As the group passed through the crowd, people began to point and whisper to each other. "Hey, that must be them!" "Are those the dogs?" "Yes, they must be, aren't those security people with them?" "Sure it is, look at that!" As the crew of the two agents, the New Yorker, the Rasta man and two dachshunds made their way up the corridor, people began to clap. First it was just a couple of isolated hands slapping together. Then a few more. And more. The sound rose into an ear shattering crescendo of applause. Someone must have recognized the heritage of Redstripe and Paris and began to shout. It turned into a chant as loud as the clapping.

"WAY TO GO WEINERS! WAY TO GO WEINERS! WAY TO GO WEINERS!"

Redstripe and Paris tried to bury their noses deep in the armpits of the agents. Sheila could not walk fast enough and Cirtron was beginning to sweat. They made it, however, to the security checkpoint at the beginning of the concourse, but it was there, not being allowed in with the ticketed passengers, that the media waited. One of the agents motioned everyone to stop. "Slight change of plans," he said calmly. "Mr. Cirtron, sir, here, you take this dog and follow right behind me. Hold it tight with two arms, okay? I need my hands free." He spoke to the other agent. "You're at the end. Mrs. Armstead, ma'am? You're right behind Mr. Cirtron." He waited to see if everyone understood and then said. "Good enough. Here we go boys and girls."

The lead agent was not polite. He just shoved his way through the crowd of reporters and camera people with his charges right behind. No one fell when his hand was planted on the chest of one or two men, even one woman, but cameras and microphones were slapped aside and a few of those hit the carpet. The agent in the rear had only his shoulders to use to push people aside as he had one of the hounds clasped to his chest. The dachshunds held tight and decided this was not a time for brash behavior.

They all got through. The Divisonal Offices of the FBI in Chicago would receive letters from disgruntled editors, but they would be ignored.

The agents finally delivered their charges to another gate on another concourse. They handed Cirtron and Sheila boarding passes, more papers for the dogs, bid them well and escorted them all the way down the causeway into the plane. The agents stopped at the doorway to the plane. One simply said, "Good luck, you'll be fine from here out. Things will be taken care of for you on the other end."

Sheila leaned over and kissed each agent on the cheek and said, "Thank you. I don't know what to say."

Cirtron raised a fist and said, "Ya, mon. Go wid GA!"

The dachshunds, released and down on the flooring, looked up and barked.

The agents looked at each other, shrugged, turned to the travelers and said, "No problem, ma'am, sir." They turned and left but not before one of them bent down and scratched the ears of both hounds.

Four leather clad seats in the first class cabin of the aircraft had been reserved for the two humans and the two hounds. Later, there would be dinner and wine on china with real knives and forks, the main course and other tidbits shared with Redstripe and Paris. Sheila and Cirtron sank into their own seats and the flight attendants fussed over the two dachshunds, petting them and using blankets to make them little nests, each in their own first class seat. The two humans were asleep before the plane reached its cruising altitude and Paris and Redstripe had already left their own nests, opting to crawl up with Cirtron, both sinking into a deep snooze. It was unbelievable, maybe, but they'd had enough fun for one day.

The landing at Montego Bay lay ahead of them all and there would plenty of new adventures to be had after everybody was rested.

Epilogue

Redstripe's Inn—Negril

We'd been sitting around a rickety table with Red Stripe beers in hand while we listened to the new stories. After I'd met Cirtron on the beach and returned to Jill to tell her about it we'd both gone over in the late afternoon to the Redstripe's Inn to hear the latest. Cirtron had finally wound down. We'd all missed the sunset so famous in Negril. But after the tales, Jill and I still were left wondering how the dogs and Sheila and Cirtron had come to be at the Redstripe's Inn. He'd ended his tale at the Chicago Airport and the transition from bison ranchers to rooming house hosts was a mystery. "Cirtron," asked Jill, "um, how did you all end up here, at the Redstripe's Inn, I mean."

I went on wondering in silence, still trying to digest the stories, about the wisdom of taking on the place. Looking around, I had lots of questions like: would the roof fall in on my head right away or would that be later?

It was Sheila who replied and answered, "We sold the farm, the ranch, deposited the bucks in the Nova Scotia Bank here in Negril and then just bought this place. Cirtron knew about it; it was for sale, so we just went ahead and did it. We haven't had much business, there is some, not a lot, but we have plenty of money left over to see us through. We do get guests but we hope for more later on."

I was still wondering. *Plenty of money to see them through?* The place was a mess. The electrical wiring looked pretty scary and the paint on the walls was peeling like the aftermath of a bad sunburn. Where the concrete blocks used to build the walls were bare, portions could be seen to be crumbling. During the day I was sure I would be able to see light seeping through the mortar joints. It would take a lot of money and effort to put the place back together. Compared to this project, Humpty Dumpty would have been a snap. And that wasn't even considering the jungle foliage outside the building that was making a concerted effort to reclaim the entire place. In a real estate ad it would not have been listed as a 'handyman's special.' It would have to be described as a 'handyman's horrendous nightmare.' I had to ask.

"But this place, you've got a great name for it, I love it, but it really needs some work. I don't mean to be rude, but are you two sure you can make this go? From what I've seen, I wouldn't even know where to start."

Redstripe and Paris had wandered in from somewhere or other and began to circle and snuffle around Sheila's ankles. She did not answer right away and just reached down to scratch two pairs of dachshund ears. The hounds rotated their heads back and forth in order to present the exact itchy parts for Sheila's fingers. Paris yawned widely with a little squeak for emphasis.

"Well," said Sheila straightening up from her hound scratching, "You're right." She looked over at Cirtron. "And I'm afraid Cirtron's talents don't fall into the fix it up category. As for me, a paintbrush in my hand is a dangerous weapon. We know we are going to need some major help."

Jill, I suppose, spoke without thinking. She certainly did not conference with me before she said, "Jack could help. He's pretty good at almost everything. I always tell him that he's a Jack of all Trades." She laughed and I cringed. Yes, I'd spent some of my former lives as an electrician, carpenter, bartender, janitor and other things that were more academic, but I had the sudden sinking feeling that I'd just been contracted out to a sure fail project.

"Really?" asked Sheila with a grin on her face.

"Yes, mon?" responded Cirtron. "You could bring y'selves here and we do it all in de family way, all t'gether? Fix up de Redstripe's Inn?"

I stared at Jill, who was still laughing, and took a look around the place once more; seeing the peeling paint, crumbling concrete and sagging roof and said, "Oh boy. I don't know about that. To move us down here for a long time? It will take a while to get this place in shape, the money to do it not withstanding and, man, I just don't know."

The dogs, Redstripe and Paris, had seated themselves on their backsides on the floor and were looking up at me. The three humans looked at me too. The idea was intriguing, I had to admit, but the problems were severe. Just moving us, even for a period of six months, to Negril would be complex. Interesting or not, I had to underscore my misgivings and said, "What would we do with Belle, our dachshund?"

Sheila had the answer all ready. "No problem, I can call Carson. She can fix it so Belle can come here, then we'd have a regular herd of hounds." Redstripe and Paris tuned into this and began to bark. *Yeah, Yeah, the more the merrier!*

I looked at the expectant faces, two canine and three human. I tried to wiggle just a bit out of a commitment and said, "Let me think about this. I believe it needs some thought. For now, though, while I am considering, you understand, I would really like another Red Stripe, please."

Printed in the United States
65081LVS00004B/183

9 781588 320940